James Relly

Epistles: or, The great salvation contemplated

In a series of letters to a Christian society

James Relly

Epistles: or, The great salvation contemplated
In a series of letters to a Christian society

ISBN/EAN: 9783741198878

Manufactured in Europe, USA, Canada, Australia, Japa

Cover: Foto ©Andreas Hilbeck / pixelio.de

Manufactured and distributed by brebook publishing software
(www.brebook.com)

James Relly

Epistles: or, The great salvation contemplated

EPISTLES:

OR,

THE GREAT SALVATION

CONTEMPLATED;

IN

A SERIES OF LETTERS

TO

A CHRISTIAN SOCIETY.

By J. R.

Glory to God in the higheſt and on earth peace, good-will
  towards men, Luke ii. 14.
What ſhall we, then, ſay to theſe things? If God be for us,
  who can be againſt us? Rom. viii. 31.
Who will have all men to be ſaved, and to come to the knowledge of the truth, 1 Tim. ii. 4.

LONDON:

Printed by M. Lewis, for the Author.

M. DCC. LXXVI.

EPISTLES:

OR,

THE GREAT SALVATION

CONTEMPLATED.

LETTER I

DEAR BRETHREN,

I T Grieved me to hear that there were difputings among you, being aware of their evil tendency; but, when the fruit appeared in the lofs of your chriftian fimplicity, it made me unhappy indeed. Alas! how deftructive to the pure and peaceable fpirit of the gofpel, is flefhly opinionative knowledge!

A 2 MORE

MORE than twelve months are elapſed, ſince I was firſt informed of your mutual heats, and trials of ſkill, reſpecting knowledge, argument and orthodoxy; during which, I have written ſundry letters to you, without taking the leaſt notice of your diſſenſions in opinion.

FROM knowledge of human nature I was aware, that my interfering in your diſputes at that time would be adding fuel to fire, and would operate as an inflammative in a fever: hence I waited for a favorable criſis, for a happy period, when I might interpoſe with advantage; but this I could not expect, until both parties were reduced to reverence truth alone, though at the expence of the darling, and to the notorious mortification of the ſelfiſh principle.

I THANK God our Saviour, I have not waited in vain: I have now the pleaſure to find you united again in that one grand and only intereſting ſubject, Jeſus Chriſt and him crucified: and

and that you are mutually influenced to lay afide fuch peculiar tenets or dogmas, as have, for fome time paft, diftinguifhed your parties; joining in chriftian fincerity, to worfhip God in the Spirit, to rejoice in Chrift Jefus, having no more confidence in the flefh. Under this influence may your fouls abide, as they will profper.

In your laft letter, unto which you all fubfcribed, you affure me, that you are perfectly fatisfied with the great falvation, rejoicing in its freenefs and fulnefs: intent alone on knowing and enjoying your perfonal intereft and happinefs therein, without the enquiry, Lord, what fhall this man do? I cannot but applaud your fpirit and conduct; may you perfevere therein to the end.

In reply to your defire (that I would give you my thoughts, according to the fcriptures, on the fubjects which fo lately diftracted you) I have no objection to communicate to you all that is

in

in my heart concerning thefe matters. But are you prepared to hear it? Are not your late divifions on thefe accounts rather too recent? May not the former fpirit and temper, in fome meafure, recur, from my attempting a folution of what formerly gave birth to them? You tell me, that your fatisfaction and rejoicing in Jefus Chrift is fuch, that whether *all*, or only a *part* of the human race, fhall be faved, is a point now of the uttermoft indifference to you ; and that the lights which the fcriptures throw on thefe doctrines, will not again confound nor dazzle your chriftian eye.

Be it fo. But in fpeaking of the fulnefs, freenefs, and extent of the great falvation, let me premife, that the two former are more immediately neceffary to be known and believed by us : for on the belief and experience of thefe depend our confolations ; whereas, whether all mankind will be faved, or not, is, among chriftians, rather a queftion of curiofity than of neceffity. Hence, I declare, that the rejoicing

which

which I have in Chriſt Jeſus, neither depends
on, nor connects *with*, either ſide of the queſtion;
but hath its foundation, riſe and ſupport, in
the report and teſtimony of the Spirit, ſpeaking
by the prophets and apoſtles, concerning Jeſus
Chriſt, and his free and full ſalvation. Therefore, ſhould I be miſtaken in my ideas, reſpecting the extent of the ſalvation of Chriſt, yet,
this miſtake cannot in the leaſt affect my own
intereſt or rejoicing in that ſalvation; nor can
I be diſtreſſed, or greatly *diſappointed*, at the de-
tection of error in ſuch opinions, as I neither
derived nor expected comfort from.

On the face of the letter, there are, in the
holy ſcriptures, three doctrines which, to a
literal view, are notoriouſly repugnant to each
other; and theſe occaſion no ſmall buſtle and
diſputations among the religious part of mankind: for when men are influenced by either of
theſe doctrines, they conclude themſelves under
obligation to militate againſt the others; and
this is one of the principal cauſes of alterca-
tion,

tion, and of diffenfions fo prevailing among chriftians.

First, There is a conditional falvation, dependent on man's repentance, faith and obedience. Secondly, There is a free and unconditional falvation of mankind, not dependent on works of righteoufnefs, as wrought by them; but this, from God's abfolute will and pleafure, is limited to a few only whom he has loved and made choice of for that purpofe; while the others, which are by far the greater part of mankind, are, by the fame will and pleafure, rejected, and excluded from that falvation. Thirdly, A general or univerfal falvation, where all, who died in Adam, fhall be made alive in Chrift.

To fuch, who, in fimplicity and chriftian candor, are converfant with the facred book, I need go no further for proof, than barely to mention it; that thefe doctrines, fo apparently contradictory, fo diametrically oppofite, are, neverthelefs, contained in that book; and to this,

the

the different profeffions of chriftians bear witnefs : for, while in particular they explode
and deny my affertion, yet, as they are Calvinifts, Arminians, or Univerfalifts, they confirm it: and, with a general voice affirm, what,
as particular fects, they deny with abhorrence.

NOTWITHSTANDING which, there are but few
individuals, fo crucified to fyftem, fo detached
from party, as to fee and confefs this truth ;
much lefs can they perceive, how thofe doctrines, fo feemingly contradictory, and oppofite to each other, fhould yet be one in Chrift,
and preaching the fame falvation, in the fame
language Yet in this light I view them, and
hope to fpeak intelligibly of the matter to you
in my next ; recommending myfelf to your
efteem, I conclude, with affuring you that I
am, in fincerity,

Your affectionate Brother and Servant,

(for Chrift's Sake)

J. R.

B   L E T-

LETTER II.

CHRIST Jefus, our Lord, is, in the holy
fcriptures, eminently called the Truth.
Every work and word of God, are only fhadowy
of him : Chrift, as the one only truth, is the
confiftence and harmony of all the feeming
contradictions contained in the fcriptures : he
hath believed and obeyed, and therefore inherits the promife :—While the people, as
united to him, as gathering with him, are, with
him, partakers of the fame falvation :—All
the promifes of God being, in him, Yea and
Amen, to them :—Jefus, as our fore-runner,
is the elect, precious, the predeftinated to eternal
life ; and fuch are the *people* in *him* :   He took

not

not on him angels, but he took on him the feed of Abraham : This is their election. Chrift alſo ſuſtained the reprobate character, when made ſin for us, and when encompaſſed with the ſorrows of death, and the pains of hell. And as to univerſal ſalvation : He is alſo the truth of that. For, though we ſee not yet all the individuals of Adam's race, as ſuch, brought up, through the knowledge of Chriſt, to the great ſalvation ; yet, in him, all fleſh have ſeen the ſalvation of God : in him, all are taught of God : in him, all know God, from the greateſt to the leaſt. In him, the whole earth is filled with the knowledge of the glory of God, as the waters cover the ſea.

But, to explain this more according to reaſon and argument, I would obſerve ; that not only the term Salvation, but every other term relating to the thing itſelf, has divers ſignifications in the ſcriptures : yet, with conſiſtence of matter, and harmony of ſpirit. To inſtance—By ſalvation, we underſtand that

      ſtate

ftate and condition in which Jefus Chrift, by
the purity of his life, the intention of his death,
and the power of his refurrection, hath placed
mankind before the face of God. This ftate
is called in the fcriptures, an everlafting falvation; the great falvation; eternal falvation;
and is defcribed as wrought in the Lord; in-
dependent of knowledge, faith, or obedience,
on the part of the faved, individually confidered; " God was, in Chrift, reconciling the
world unto himfelf, not imputing their tref-
paffes unto them." In this falvation, God beholds us without fpot, or blemifh, or any fuch
thing: Our iniquities are pardoned, our warfare is accomplifhed; fo that the Lord be-
holdeth no iniquity in Jacob, nor perverfenefs
in Ifrael. This is the falvation, in which God
ever beholds his creatures, and which the gofpel
preaches to them as glad tidings, that faith
might come by hearing.

AGAIN, Salvation, fometimes in the fcriptures, is made to depend on our repentance,
belief,

belief, and obedience. This I might explain
in a twofold fenfe ; either as the voice of the
law, in contradiftinction to the free unconditional gofpel-falvation, fpoken of above ; or,
as relating to the knowledge and joy of that
free falvation ; a proper explication in either
fenfe, would be true : But, to abide by the
fubject in hand, I wave the firft, and adhere to
the fecond.

THIS falvation diftinguifhes the perfon who
believeth on Jefus, from him who believeth
not ; and, in a gofpel fenfe, is defcribed, as
the happy confequence, the only and bleffed
fruit of believing the report concerning Jefus
Chrift : i. e. that he is, before God, our free,
perfect, and eternal falvation. It confifts in a
peculiar ftate of mind, an exemption from
guilt, fin and fear, a poffeffion of righteoufnefs,
peace and joy in the Holy Ghoft. This is not
only to have bread enough in our Father's
houfe, but to fit down alfo at his table and
eat : This falvation may be inftantaneous or
gradual,

gradual, as it pleafes God to reveal his Son
in us.

THIS falvation, as I hinted before, is obtained, on condition of believing and obeying
the truth : nor does it follow, that becaufe
faith is the gift of God, and obedience the influence of his free Spirit, that thefe are not
conditional ; fince we are active in both, our
faculties are in exercife in believing and obeying : Hence, " with the heart man believeth
unto righteoufnefs, and, with the mouth, confeffion is made unto falvation :" And, until
we have this belief and confeffion, we attain
not to falvation in the above fenfe.

IN a firft fenfe, Repentance, faith and obedience, are what conftitute the everlafting
righteoufnefs of our Lord Jefus Chrift : his
repentance confifted of ftrong cries and tears,
of the broken heart, and contrite fpirit : his
deep inexplicable humiliations—fuch as were
heard in that he feared—fuch as were rewarded
with

with the higheſt name, and the moſt glorious
exaltation : his faith conſiſted in believing the
promiſes, which were all made to him : and
theſe he believed, through all the moſt diſ-
couraging ſcenes of life and death ; even when
the terrors of death encompaſſed him, and
the pains of hell gat hold on him : And when
his faith was perfected by his works.

THE obedience of our Lord Jeſus Chriſt,
is uſually diſtinguiſhed into active and paſſive.
The one implying his immaculate life, and the
other his ſubmiſſion to ſufferings, and his obedience to death : all which infinite purity approved of, juſtifying him in the ſpirit of holineſs, and declaring him the Author of ſalvation.

THESE, the Saviour, from the ſucceſs of his
undertakings, and his exaltation in conſequence
thereof, hath full power to reckon over, impute
or give to the children of men ; " for him
hath God exalted with his own right hand, to
be

be a Prince and a Saviour, to give repentance unto Ifrael, and remiffion of fin."

OUR Saviour's repentance, faith, and obedience, are perfect and permanent : but our repentance, faith, and obedience, are neither perfect, nor permanent. But, as that which is perfect, is neceffary to give us confidence towards God, he gives us *his* repentance, faith, and obedience : and when that which is perfect is come, that which is in part only is done away. We no longer depend *on* or gather *with* our own repentances, obedience, and faith. The utmoft that our faith, or the faith which is in us, can attain to, is to believe, receive, and appropriate, according to his will, the faith, repentance, and obedience of Chrift ; and in thefe we find falvation.

BUT, though it be true, that we know in part, fee but in part ; yet to experience and rejoice in this falvation, it is neceffary that we fhould know and fee in our meafure.

For

meafure. For it is eafily feen, that, except we are perfonally poffeffed of faith, we can neither believe, know, nor appropriate the faith of Chrift. Hence the neceffity of faith in us to this falvation; as there is of eating, to the man who (having bread in his houfe) would fill his belly therewith.

Repentance, as it refpects the exercife and feelings of the human heart, confifts of conviction, compunction, and renovation. Light breaks in upon the mind, difcovering to us the error of our ways, and the infufficiency of all our own righteoufnefs: Compunction of heart follows, for the deception we have been under, and for the yet corrupt bias of our fpoiled nature: we loath, abhor, and deteft ourfelves, for what we feel: more efpecially for that vile propenfity which is in us (notwithftanding the vicioufnefs and poverty of our nature) to truft in ourfelves, and in our own righteoufneffes; in oppofition to the free-grace and falvation of our Lord Jefus Chrift; whom now we lan-

C

guifh

guiſh for, and pant to have every thought
brought into captivity to his obedience, count-
ing all things as loſs, yea, but dung, that we
may win Chriſt, and be found in him ; not having our own righteouſneſs. Theſe particulars
manifeſt a change, a renewal ; but this change,
this renewal, withſtands and over-rules our
original bias, not permitting us to look for
righteouſneſs and ſtrength into ourſelves, but
inclines us to Jeſus, in whom we have everlaſting righteouſneſs, and invincible ſtrength.

In brief, the ſalvation promiſed in the ſcriptures, on condition of believing, obeying, &c.
is, that bleſſed and happy ſtate of mind, which
is the aſſured fruit and conſequence of knowing, believing, and obeying Jeſus Chriſt, as the
great, finiſhed, eternal, unchangeable ſalvation :
which ſtate conſiſts of righteouſneſs, purity,
peace, joy, and full aſſurance of everlaſting
life. This is a ſalvation : for we are here ſaved
from ſin, guilt, war, diſtreſs, and fear : not
phyſically, as though we were not yet men
                                        ſubject

subject to like passions with others, but legally
and imputatively, as the man is saved whose
debts are paid, and whose crimes are cancelled, by an equal chastisement ; and withal,
conscientiously : for the gospel teaches, and we
believe, that Jesus Christ, through the whole of
his obedience, active and passive, and in all
that he obtained thereby, was still considered
as those whom he came into the world to save.
Hence we have an undoubted right to believe,
that we are freed from sin and condemnation ;
and that he hath presented us to himself a glorious church, not having spot or wrinkle, or any
such thing ; but that we should be holy and
without blemish. If our heart live in contact
with this truth, we have, in perfect peace and
purity, compleat salvation in Jesus ; without
works of righteousness, as done by us, individually considered ; as saith the apostle, "But
to him that worketh not, but believeth on him
that justifieth the ungodly, his faith is counted
for righteousness." Obedience here, consists
in an entire submission to the will of God, as

thus

thus revealed and executed in Chrift Jefus; without attempting, by what *we* may do or fuffer, to recommend ourfelves to the divine favor, or to qualify ourfelves for the reception of it, or to make adequate returns for the bleffings received. Thus is Chrift the author of eternal falvation, unto all them that obey him.—Of ourfelves we are nothing, we have nothing, we can do nothing—but, eating him, we live by him. On the above condition, we have, we inherit, we enjoy the falvation of God, by Jefus Chrift.

Thus would I underftand and explain conditional falvation, as taught in the fcriptures; as what refpects the ftate of believers only, in the ages of time; and not that reft which yet remaineth for the people of God, that final determinate falvation, which God has decreed, and which Jefus has perfected, and ordained, to be the eternal ftate of man. What influence this falvation has on the mind, is better felt and enjoyed, than explained: nor are there

any

any other means of attaining to it, than the faith and obedience already defcribed : May the teftimony of Jefus, by the hearing of which they come, produce and maintain them in all your hearts. This is the prayer and defire of

Your Brother and Servant,

(for Chrift's fake)

J. R.

LETTER III.

DEAR BRETHREN,

I DO not pretend to have given you, in my laſt letter, a perfect copy of the Arminian creed ; nay, I am well aware of the contrary. I know, that inſtead of our own works of righteouſneſs and creature actings, which *they* make to be the conditions of ſalvation ; *I* ſubſtitute a total ceſſation from all dependence and hope on theſe : and a ſimple unreſerved ſubmiſſion to Chriſt. Nor are we agreed, on the *object* of our faith and obedience.—*I*, profeſſing all things that are written in the ſcriptures, believe, that it is not in the nature of man to *do*, nor even to *will*, what is good, and accords with the will of God. I muſt therefore always conclude it a

fatal

fatal miftake, proceeding from the groffeft ignorance of themfelves, of the fcriptures, and
of the power of God ; for men to pretend, to
will and *power* in *themfelves* to do what can fave
them, either in the whole or in part ; or even
recommend them to the favor of God, or
qualify them for its reception. Man, thus confidered, I believe that God reconciled him to
himfelf in Jefus Chrift, who in our nature,
name, and perfons, fulfilled all righteoufnefs,
and inherited the promife : Hence, that glorious
record, "God hath given to us eternal life,
and that life is in his Son." He hath given it
to us, not as righteous perfons, but as finners ;
not to us as believers, but as unbelievers ; not
to us as obedient, but as difobedient. Nor
does man's unbelief and refufal of the gift of
God, make void *his* eternal donation, whofe
gifts and callings are without repentance : for
if God alter his purpofe of mercy and grace
towards men, and recall the gift of eternal life,
which he hath given them in his Son ; then is
their unbelief no longer culpable, nay, it is no

longer

longer unbelief, but an uncenfurable fentiment.
But while unbelief is iniquity, whilft fuch who
are under its influence, blafphemoufly, yet
with impunity, give the lye to God ; the grace
which is oppofed muft certainly remain per-
manently free, full, and glorious. Hence, we
fight, not as though we beat the air ; nor do
we preach uncertainties to man : we hold forth
to them a finifhed falvation, a glorious reft remaining for them in Chrift Jefus : into the glory
and riches of which, nothing but their difobedience or unbelief prevents their entrance.

Undoubtedly, this is the hearing by which
faith cometh ; it is wifely and gracioufly
adapted to the heiplefs ftate of man. But O !
how widely different is this from the faith of
fuch, who make man's righteoufnefs the condition of falvation, they know not the helplefs
ftate of the creature, nor that he is indeed fub-
jefted to vanity. Hence, they fee no reafon
wherefore their falvation fhould be finifhed and
fecured in Chrift. They believe it not ; it is a
doftrine repugnant to their hope and defire,

and

and therefore they generally meet and encounter it with hatred or derifion.

LIKE the old Egyptian tafk-mafters, they call on you to make your tale of bricks, without allowing you proper materials : they call on you to obey, without communicating fufficiency, or even giving you a certain invariable rule for the extent, nature, and properties of true obedience. When they fpeak of believing, they acknowledge no truth until it is believed, nor a Chrift, until he is applied. Hence, that very abfurd faying, fo frequent in the mouth and writings of fome, who would be thought to be minifters of the gofpel, "An unapplied Chrift, is no Chrift at all."

BUT, I need not yet take pains to fhew you, that, by conditional falvation, I underftand prefent falvation, or the falvation of Chrift, enjoyed in this life : the conditions of obtaining and rejoicing in which, are undoubtedly faith and obedience; for, if we believe it not, we

D   poffefs

possess it not : and if we obey it not, we rejoice not in it : yet this faith and obedience, are the free gift of him " who worketh in us to will and to do of his own good pleasure." The apostle, speaking of faith, tells us, that it " comes by hearing, and hearing by the word of God." By affirming and illustrating the truth, and persuading men that they have, in Jesus, the forgiveness of sin : that they are saved in him, justified in him, sanctified and preserved in him : until, believing it unto righteousness, and confessing it unto salvation, they rejoice in him with joy unspeakable, and full of glory.

HENCE, Salvation spoken of, and described in this manner, perfectly consists, not only with the free unconditional salvation of the elect ; but even with the doctrine of *universal* salvation : when we distinguish between a finished salvation, the present enjoyment, and a future enjoyment.

THE

THE elect, where applied to the persons of mankind, in subordination to Christ, intends such, who are made choice of in time to the belief of the truth, and the joy of salvation.

THESE are chosen to this grace, not on the consideration of present, nor on the foresight of future merit in themselves : but he, whom they sought not, is pleased to be found of them : Yea, left aught should be placed to the account of human righteousness, the unerring Spirit has thus drawn the character of the chosen—"Not many wise men, after the flesh ; not many mighty, not many noble ; but God hath chosen the foolish, the weak, the base, the despised :" And the reason, which he has vouchsafed to give for his choice, is, " That no flesh should glory in his presence; but he that glorieth should glory in the Lord."

HENCE, I propose, that the elect are not a people chosen to be the objects of God's love and salvation, to the final exclusion of others :

D 2

but

but a people chofen to believe the truth, and to rejoice in the falvation of Jefus in time ; while others yet remain in a ftate of ignorance, of what they are equally entitled to with the elect.

THE elect, who are predeftinated to the prefent knowledge, and enjoyment of eternal life, can only attain to this happinefs through faith and obedience, as fpoken of before, under the article of conditional falvation. But, as Chrift effects this in them, by his gofpel and free fpirit, it comes not, as I have hinted before, under the imputation of man's righteoufnefs : nor is it a denial to the elect's being freely faved, fince what a man poffeffes without coft to himfelf, is free to him.

SHOULD it be afked, What advantage have the elect above others ? I anfwer, Much every way : For " one day in his courts, is better than a thoufand in the tents of wickednefs ; the fecret of the Lord is with them ; he hath

shewed

shewed them his covenant : They have righteousness, peace, and joy in the Holy Ghost:
Through all the viciffitudes of life, and in
death, they have affurance of eternal life.

If the fcriptures afcribe Predeftination and
Election to the fovereignty of God, they clafh
not with my idea of it : fince there can be none
other reafon affigned, for his choofing one
rather than another, to the belief and enjoyment
of the truth, than his fovereign will and pleafure.

Do the facred writings afcribe their election,
&c. to free grace of God ? This alfo corre-
fponds with the hints abovementioned, as appears from the character of whom he hath
chofen ; and alfo from his manner in bringing
them to the knowledge of the truth.

According to this idea of Election, the con-
fiftency, and even the expediency of the apoftle's exhortation, is perceivable : " Give all
diligence,

diligence, to make your calling and election sure :" And, again, " Put on, as the elect of God, bowels of mercy, long-suffering," &c.

ELECTION and Predestination, thus considered, are no denial to salvation finished for all, in the person of Christ; nor is it an objection to the future final happiness of all; for whom Christ died : nay, it rather supposes it; if the predestinate and elect are so called, from their being chosen to believe, and enjoy in time, what the residue neither know, nor enjoy but in eternity. But, as I purpose, towards the close of these letters, to explain myself more fully on this subject, I shall wave a further explanation of it here, to observe—That, in my first letters, I intended only a few hints to you, which I judged necessary to prepare the way to the subject on which, in particular, you desired to know my mind. Therefore, my intention is, in a few letters, to confine myself to the subject of God's universal love and salvation in Jesus Christ. I am not aware of any hurt to
your

your minds, that can proceed from it, if you are indeed fatisfied with Chrift; being well perfuaded, that if you are really affured of the freenefs of his falvation, you will no more enter into doubtful and flefhly difputations, concerning the extent of it.

MAY Jefus Chrift, the Apoftle and High-Prieft of our profeffion, render it more than an amufement to you! May he ufe it to endear his name, perfon, falvation, and Spirit to you! Such is the Prayer and defire of,

Yours, &c.

J. R.

LETTER IV.

WHEN we read the facred book, let our hearts feel none other bias, than the glory of Chrift alone ; to teftify of whom, the unerring Spirit dictated what the prophets and apoftles wrote.

IF thus qualified, we inveftigate truth ; we fhall quickly perceive, that the love of God, and the falvation of Jefus, are, in their freenefs and extent, infinitely beyond what the ancient Jews, or even the generality of modern chriftians, have apprehended.

IN

In the book we read, that "God is love:" that he hath so loved the world as to give his only beloved Son for the life of it; and that his Son has died for the sins of the whole world : From whence we may infer, that no man is excluded from the love of God, or from the salvation of Christ.

With what propriety can it be conceived, that God should create beings under an unavoidable destiny to sin, and endless misery ? Does it consist with the righteousness and equity of the divine nature ? does it consist with the warnings, calls, invitations, and reproofs, wherewith he has admonished men from the beginning ? Is it compatible with his promises ? or even with the threatenings, where the sinner and the ungodly are threatened ? Nay, God our Father has taught us the reverse ; where he has sworn by his life, that he desireth not the death of a sinner, but that he should turn from his wickedness, and· live. Who are decreed and created to destruction, cannot be said to be condemned for their own demerits, but

E. ·   for

for the sole pleasure of God ; but, than this, there is nothing more untrue.

WILL divine Justice censure men for not believing a lye ? for not believing what they never had a right to believe ; yea, what was never true to them ? Will God the Judge of all men, destroy his creatures for not doing what he never gave them abilities for ; yea, for not doing, what he decreed they should not do? Is our Father, Redeemer, and Saviour, such an austere master, as to expect to gather, where he has not strewed, and to reap where he has not sowed ?

HE, who hath seen and declared the Father, and who only hath seen and declared him, has taught us, that God loved the world, yea so loved it, as to give the Son of his bosom ; than whom, as given for the life of the world, heaven had not, in all its treasures, a richer gift, a higher and more incontestable evidence, of his love and good-will towards man. " And, if God hath not spared his own Son, but hath delivered him up for us all, how shall he not, with him, freely give us all things ?".   WHO

WHO, that has tafted that God is gracious; who, that has confidered his loving-kindnefs, can yet hefitate to believe, that God is good and gracious unto every man ; yea, that his great good will extends to the children of men univerfally, without refpect of perfons ?

WHEN I behold the glory of the Son of man, the dignity of his perfon, the intention of his obedience and fufferings, the immenfity of his blood, and the power and purity of his refurrection, I am ecftafied ! I cannot with-hold, but am conftrained to cry out, O ! amazing grace ! " where fin hath abounded, grace hath much more abounded." What are the iniquities of a thoufand worlds ! O Zion, what are all thy tranfgreffions, though numberlefs ; when thy God deigns to purchafe thee with his own blood ! What are the complicated fins of a guilty world, to this great and glorious falvation ! The demerit of the one, to the merit of the other, bears no more proportion than a pearly drop of morning dew to the deep and

wide extended ocean ; or than a duſt of the
balance, to the terreſtrial globe : yea, the re-
quiſites to man's deliverance from ſin, and from
all its conſequences, bear not more proportion
to that glorious deliverance, as wrought in and
by Jeſus Chriſt our Lord ; than a moment of
time to the ages of eternity.   Such are the
aboundings of God's everlaſting grace ! ſuch
the divinity of our Saviour's blood and righteouſneſs !

Who can ſee this, and yet ſtart at the ex-
preſſion—" All fleſh ſhall ſee his ſalvation ?"
Who can behold this, and yet be anxious to
find out, among the individuals of Adam's
race, ſuch whom they may exclude from ſalvation, ſo free and extenſive as is that of our
Lord Jeſus Chriſt ?

But, to avoid the imputation of an attempt
to impoſe on the judgment, by an addreſs to
the paſſions, I ſhall proceed to collect a few of
the moſt remarkable paſſages in the book,
                                    ſpeak-

speaking of the general love and good-will
of God to mankind : shewing, by the way,
the relation they stand in to the hypothesis of
universal salvation. My intention is, next, to
examine with candour, and ingenuously to reply, to what wears the face of the most ma-
terial objections to this doctrine.

" IN thy feed shall all the nations of the
earth be blessed," Gen. xxiii. 18. which feed is
Christ, saith the apostle. The sum of which is,
that all the nations of the earth shall be blessed
in Christ. Nor does the text, to a simple and
unprejudiced mind, need a comment. Nor
shall I spend my time here, to shew the impro-
priety of such comments, as pretend, that
" all the nations of the earth," intend only
various nations ; or a few individuals out of all
these various nations ; or that the blessing,
promised to all nations in Christ, intends the
good example only, which they have in him ;
or the good instructions he has given them ; or,
the possibility of salvation for them, on such, or

such

such terms ; or the temporal blessings which all possess through him ; with many more such like human inventions, calculated to evade the force of the promise, and to limit its grace; since, but to mention these, is to expose their absurdity.

But, as I believe, that God our Saviour meant not to trifle with his creatures, but to fulfil his promises to them ; so am I persuaded that he meant to speak to their understanding and common sense, in all his promises : and not to propose theses for trials of skill, at logic, rhetoric, and sophistry. Hence, when I hear him say, *all the nations of the earth*, I readily conclude that he intended, not only all the nations inheriting the earth at some particular period ; but all that the earth hath contained from the beginning, or shall contain, to the end of time.

When I hear God himself promise a blessing to mankind, my mind immediately conceives of somewhat very different from a curse : but if men are not blessed with eternal life, it is

easily

eafily proved, that all other bleffings, fo called, terminate in a curfe.

WHEN I hear it promifed, that this bleffing fhould be in Chrift, I readily conclude, that it is not in man: and can therefore conceive, how men may be bleffed in Chrift, though they may be ignorant of it in themfelves.

IN *thy feed fhall all the nations of the earth be bleffed.* This is not only defcriptive of God's method of bleffing mankind, i. e. in Chrift ; but it alfo denotes the continuance of the blefs-ing. It is not in man, who is given to change, but it is in him, who is the *fame, yefterday, to-day, and for ever.* Though all the nations be dead, yet the bleffing, their eternal life, is hid with Chrift in God ; where it is fo well fecured, that they may not, by any means, be deprived of it. Nor is their prefent ignorance a proof that they fhall not, in fome future period, pof-fefs ; and rejoice in the bleffing, which, by the grace of God, they are entitled to.

UNTO

UNTO *thee shall all flesh come*, Psalm lxv. 2.
By all flesh, I would understand all mankind :
for to this purpose is the term, *all flesh*, made
use of, in the scriptures : as in Genesis, " *For
all flesh had corrupted his way, upon the earth*," and
in Numbers, " *He is the God of the spirits of all
flesh*," &c. So in the text, " *Unto thee shall all
flesh come*." This promise is already fulfilled,
in the person of Christ ; in whom all the promises are Yea and Amen. Jesus hath, in himself, brought up, all flesh to God ; unto whom
he hath presented them holy and irreprovable :
nor will he cease to rule, until what is true in
him, shall be true in them also : until all flesh
shall come to the knowledge and enjoyment of
his salvation.

THE *glory of the Lord shall be revealed, and all
flesh shall see it together*, Isaiah xl. 5. This was
reveal.d in Jesus Christ, who was the bright-
ness of the glory, and the express image of the
person of God : who was God manifested in

the

the flesh, so that angels were capable of seeing the Invisible.

Moses, and others in their day, were desirous of seeing his glory ; but saw it not. The glory which Moses was desirous of seeing, is called the face of God ; and may intend the nature and properties of Deity, with his purposes and designs. But though this sight was denied to Moses, yet God promised that his glory should be revealed, and that all flesh should see it together.

This promise is fulfilled in Jesus ; in him is the glory of God revealed ; and in him all flesh, i. e. all mankind were so collected, and situated, that they saw it together. As Adam, so Christ occupied all flesh, in his knowledge of the Father : he being in his office-capacity, and mystery, all flesh gathered together : his views, his enjoyments, his knowledge, are theirs ; and thus all flesh have together seen the glory of God.

F

Nor

No_r does this deny, but fuppofes ; yea, fe-cures to all flefh, a perfonal fight and enjoyment of the glory of God in fome future age ; when his glory fhall be revealed, and all flefh fhall fee it together.

A_{nd} *all flefh fhall fee the falvation of God,* Luke iii. 6 According to the fenfe of the facred book, the promife of feeing, is the pro-mife of poffeffing and enjoying : does it not follow, then, that all flefh fhall enjoy the fal-vation of God ? As the terms, *all flefh,* in af-ferting the corruption of our fpecies, manifeftly include Adam and all his offspring ; there can be no juft reafon offered, why the fame terms, when ufed in promife, fhould not have the fame latitude. Hence all mankind fhall fee, and en-joy the falvation of God.

As *by the offence of one, judgment came upon all men to condemnation ; even fo by the righteoufnefs of One, the free gift came upon all men unto juftification of life,* Rom. v. 18. To the unprejudiced mind
this

this text needs no comment: here the plaifter is manifeftly as wide as the fore—and the remedy, both in its application and benefit, as extenfive and powerful as the difeafe.

THIS text, like the pregnant comb, drops honey at the touch, and needs no preffure. Here the grace which diftinguifhes the ever adorable name, and inexplicable falvation of Jefus, fhines in its meridian luftre. Here, the amazing freenefs, and extent of love and grace, fo fparkles and fpeaks, that the mole and the bat only can be blind, and the adder deaf! Meat is here brought out of the eater, and fweetnefs out of the ftrong.

THIS text fhews us the method and freenefs of God's eternal grace, in the falvation of mankind by Jefus Chrift our Lord. " As by the offence of one, fo by the righteoufnefs of one." By the former, without their aid, concurrence, affent, or even knowledge, judgment came upon all unto condemnation: in like manner, by

the

he latter, the free gift came upon all men to juſtification of life. This is free grace indeed! here the chambers of darkneſs and death, teem with the rays and evidences of light, life, and immortality : and even the wandering ſteps of man, ſabled with guilt, and leading to judgment and condemnation, illuſtrate and perpetuate the method and freeneſs of the great ſalvation.

THE free gift came upon *all men,* unto juſtification of life.—Upon all on whom judgment came unto condemnation. Hence, it is true beyond all controverſy, that, as all Adam's offspring, by means of his offence, were brought under judgment to condemnation ; ſo it is equally true, that, by means of Chriſt's righteouſneſs, Adam and all his offspring were brought under the free gift of juſtification unto eternal life. We have moſt aſſuredly the ſame revelation of God for the one, as we have for the other.

WHAT,

WHAT, if men do not believe, shall their unbelief make the faith of God of none effect? Is their unbelief a reasonable objection to a FREE gift? or, is their unrighteousness an argument, that this free gift cannot come upon them by the righteousness of Jesus Christ? Have those words, a *gift*, a *free gift*, a *free gift of justification unto life*, coming upon all men—no meaning in them? Nay, let priest-craft, bigotry, and prejudice, sift and winnow them, their substance will yet remain: It will be for ever true, that God hath concluded all in unbelief, that he might have mercy on all.

ALL the children of Adam do not at present know, that judgment came upon them to condemnation by his offence; nay, there are thousands who deny it. But does it follow from thence, that it is not true? Quite the reverse. Their ignorance and opposition confirm the proposition, that all are dead in him. Neither does man's ignorance of it, nor even his opposition to it, indicate, that the free gift is not come

upon

upon him to juſtification of life. It is rather a proof of the free gift.

JUSTIFICATION of life, according to the words of the book, implies a perfect exemption from the charge of ſin, and conſequently from condemnation. This is juſtification: and juſtification of life, intends a juſtification of that life and impunity which they obtain as a free gift by the righteouſneſs of Chriſt : Thus is God juſt, in juſtifying the ungodly.

IF this grace be true to all, according to that great plainneſs of ſpeech uſed by the apoſtle, wherefore ſhould not all, ſooner or later, poſſeſs it ? Sin, or any impediment ariſing from thence, cannot prevent their final happineſs in this grace : becauſe the gift which came upon them, is that of juſtification : which acquits from ſin, and all its conſequences : nor can their poverty and helpleſſneſs prevent it ; becauſe it is a *free gift*, a good and *perfect* gift, which came from the Father of lights, with
whom

whom there is neither variablenefs nor fhadow
of turning : whofe gifts and callings are without repentance. From all which, I fee no reafon wherefore all men fhould not in fome future
period, be bleffed with the enjoyment of eternal
life.

For *as in Adam all die, even fo in Chrift fhall all
be made alive,* 1 Cor. xv. 22. This is a text perfectly fimilar in its language to the former, and
therefore would need none other remarks than
what I have made on the above.——But, that ex-
pofitors (in my judgment) give it a fenfe very
different from the intention of the Holy Ghoft
by the apoftle. Commentators tell us, that
as by means of Adam's offence, all men became
mortal, and muft neceffarily fee death ; fo by
means of Chrift's refurrection and power, they
fhall all be made alive, or raifed from the dead.
Unto which I anfwer, If they meant that the
all thus made alive in Chrift, or raifed from the
dead in him, were raifed to eternal life and glory, the comment would be good : but, as they
                                        intend

intend nothing lefs than this ; theirs is not the
genuine fenfe of the text, as will appear from
what follows.

THE text manifeftly oppofes Chrift and his
life, to Adam, and his death ; and fhews the
former to be as extenfive as the latter. As an
infallible medicine to a fore difeafe, as a difpenfation of comfort to a fcene of mifery ; fo is
the text adapted to the helplefs ftate of man.
Thofe blefled words contain a declaration and
promife of man's deliverance in Chrift : yea,
of all men's deliverance from the mifery or
death wherein they are involved in Adam.

BUT, wherein is the propriety of fuch a declaration, or promife, if the greater part of thofe
who are made alive in Chrift, are only made
alive for deftruction, and rendered thereby more
capable of torment ? Can they receive any
poffible advantage, in conjunction with eternal
mifery ? Is not an annihilation preferable to eternal damnation ? What profit will fuch receive

by

by being made alive in Chrift, who are made
alive to greater and endlefs mifery ? Can this
be the voice of love ? Can it be the fenfe of the
text ? If fo, the natural comment is this, For
as in Adam all die, and according to the body
mingle with the duft, and become fenfelefs as
the clay ; fo in Chrift they fhall all be made
alive : fome to the fenfe of happinefs, but (by
much) the greater part to the fenfe of everlafting torment. Except to a very few, where is
the grace, where is the falvation, propofed in
the text, agreeable to fuch a comment ?

ACCORDING to this method of explaining that
fcripture, Adam has laid the *foundation* of human mifery, and Chrift raifes the *fuperftructure.*
Adam has drank the deadly thing fo foporiferous
to all his offspring ; and Chrift makes them
alive, awakes and quickens them to inexplicable and never-ending torment. This is a notorious inverfion of the gofpel, and, according
to my idea, a blafphemy againft Chrift : who
fays, that he " came not into the world to

G   deftroy

deſtroy the wo ld, but that the world through him might have life."

THERE are others, who, though they allow that all men without diſtinction die in Adam, yet will have the *all* who are made alive in Chriſt, to be all the elect only ; who, according to them, are a very ſmall number, in compariſon of thoſe who die in Adam. Hence the phraſe often uſed, As in Adam all *his ſeed* die, even ſo in Chriſt all *his ſeed* ſhall be made alive ; as though the ſeed of Chriſt was not ſo extenſive as the ſeed of Adam. Others ſay, All who believe and obey the goſpel ſhall be made alive in Chriſt jeſus : as if, when dead, they were to believe and obey, in order to their being made alive. Merely to mention theſe comments, and others of like nature, is ſufficient to prove them a manifeſt perverſion of the ſacred text. And yet it is amazing to ſee, how greedily men ſwallow, how eagerly they adopt, the moſt ſtrained unnatural comment ; rather

than

than acknowledge fuch a freenefs and extent
of grace as the true gofpel preaches !

WHO but reads the text with a heart unprejudiced, and open to the impreffions of truth,
muft neceffarily perceive the *reality* of falvation,
the *method* and *extent* of it ? The reality of it—
They fhall be made alive in Chrift. The method
of it—As they die in Adam, fo fhall they be
made alive in Chrift. The extent of it—ALL
—"As in Adam ALL die, fo in Chrift fhall ALL
be made alive." Thus the aboundings of grace
are as extenfive as thofe of fin: and Chrift is
declared to be as univerfal in *his* falvation, as
Adam was in the ruin of mankind.

AND, left the old queftion fhould recur, i. e.
" Who will fhew us any good ?" If God has
promifed to make all alive in Chrift, how comes
it that his promife is not fulfilled, fince the
whole world yet lieth in the wicked one ? I anfwer—In Chrift the firft fruits, the promife is
already fulfilled, as it fhall be in all that are his

at his coming. All mankind are legally and
myſtically made alive in Chriſt; " who died for
their ſins, and roſe again for their juſtification."
Thus, whether we wake or ſleep, we live together
with him. The preſent ignorance and unbelief of mankind does not hinder their being
made accepted in the beloved; nor will it prevent their knowledge and enjoyment in ſome
age to come.

But here I recollect that I am writing a letter, and looking back on what I have written,
am convinced that it is already too long; ſhall
therefore conclude with ſubſcribing myſelf,

Your Brother and Servant,

(for Chriſt's Sake)

J. R.

LETTER V.

DEAR BRETHREN,

I CONCLUDED my laſt with ſome remarks on that ſacred teſtimony of the apoſtle, " As in Adam all die, ſo in Chriſt ſhall all be made alive:" I ſhall begin this with another quotation from the ſame great and glorious witneſs of Jeſus, who, ſpeaking of the infinite love of God our Saviour, ſays, " He will have all men to be ſaved, and to come to the knowledge of the truth," 1 Tim. ii. 4. Theſe words are not only expreſſive of the love of God, with the pity and tenderneſs of Emanuel's heart ; but they declare his poſitive will : " He will have all men to be ſaved, and to come to the know-

ledge

ledge of the truth." Who hath refisted his will?
It is the happiness of mankind to submit, but
their non-submission and refistance prevents not
the execution of his will.

SOME are weak enough to imagine, that the
Almighty muft firft get his creatures leave, before he can perform his will refpecting them;
hence they plume themfelves on *their* fub-
miffions, and compliment their own great humility, in being content that the will of the
Lord fhould be done. I am aware of fome
men's affecting to fay, that the text only intends
the willingnefs and defire of God our Saviour,
that all men fhould be faved, and come to the
knowledge of the truth. But, fay they, it does
not follow that all fhall be faved : becaufe the
greater part choofe death rather than life, refufe
to comply with the terms of falvation; and
thereby fruftrate God's holy will and defire.

WHAT a jumble of error and inconfiftency!
The Creator of the ends of the earth is not abfolute :

folute : he may will, yea, he may *defire* the falvation of his creatures, yet both may be frus-
trate, if the creature choofes to ftand out ; and
will neither comply with his will, nor gratify
his defire !.

God has but one choice, which is, that all
fhould be faved, and come to the knowledge of
the truth : but his creatures have power to put
a negative upon the choice of the Almighty,
whereby his will and defire are rendered of non-
effect : whereas they are abfolute and uncontroulable in *their* choice. If they choofe death
rather than life, die they muft, for the Lord
God of truth, who made them and redeemed
them, cannot prevent it ; howfoever defirous he
may be of it.

I believe I have ftated the matter fairly, according to the above : fhall therefore leave it
to you to determine of its propriety, and confonance to truth : left you fhould accufe me of
mif-fpending time and words to expofe, what
(but to fuch who are intoxicated with enmity
. and

and pride) is in itſelf moſt notoriouſly falſe, abſurd, and blaſphemous.

In the ſacred book, we read much of ſubmiſſion to the will of God; and his worſhippers have been often heard to ſay, The will of the Lord be done. But is this written, that we ſhould admire *their* humility, and condeſcenſion, in permitting God to do his will, though it ſhould be trying and grievous to them according to the fleſh? God forbid. Yea, the ſcriptures were written that man might be abaſed, and the Lord alone exalted.

The will of God our Saviour is abſolute, immutable, and irreſiſtible. The ſcriptures teach this. After many trials, poſſibly experience corroborates it. Is it then a mark of humility, ſelf-denial, or lowlineſs of heart, to ſubmit to his will, the fixed unalterable will of God, which neither men nor angels can reſiſt? Nay, there is no virtue in ſubmitting to what we cannot avoid.

THE

THE true worshipper knows, that the will of his God is determinate: hence he will no longer strive, as the potsherd of the earth, with his Maker. He is withal assured, that according to the mystery of the divine will, all things work together for his good; and therefore he not only submits, but rejoices in his will. Hence the expression, The will of the Lord be done: and the prayer which the Saviour taught his disciples, " Thy will be done on earth as it is done in heaven."

THE plain honest heart neither knows nor admits of such distinctions in the will of God, as permissive and decretive; as though, for causes arising from the capriciousness of the creature, he permitted that to be, which he had not foreseen nor decreed; or that what he had decreed, he, for like reasons, thought proper to dispense with.

To distinguish between God's prescience and his decree, favours too much of human invention and subtlety, for the simplicity of chris-

H   tianity:

tianity : known unto God are all his works.
What he foreknew, that he had decreed ; and
what he had decreed, that he permits. Foreknowledge differs not from the decree, respecting events : for as God cannot be deceived,
neither can he be controuled. The distinction,
that God's foreknowledge of all events does
not lay us under a necessity of acting, but that
his decree does ; appears to me, to be destitute
of reason and common sense : for God is infallible in his foreknowledge, as in his decree :
what he foreknew must most assuredly come to
pass : nor can there be *more* attributed to his
decree.

HAVING thus considered the will of God, as
sovereign, absolute, and uncontroulable, let us
weigh the purport of it; i. e. that all men should
be saved, and come to the knowledge of the
truth : note, the distinction between being
saved, and coming to the knowledge of the
truth. From the remarks already made, it is
evident, that all men are saved in Christ Jesus

the

the Lord, with an everlafting falvation : but all
men are not yet come to the knowledge of the
truth ; neverthelefs, he who willed the former,
and executed it, according to the purpofe of his
will, hath alfo willed the latter, and according
to the fame purpofe will execute it in his own
times ; when all men fhall come to the knowledge of the truth.

AGAIN, " Who gave himfelf a ranfom for all,
to be teftified in due time," 1 Tim. ii. 6. In
that God our Saviour gave *himfelf*, he hath given
us an infallible proof of divine love. He hath
given himfelf *unto* and *for* all : and hath here-
by made manifeft the extent of divine grace.
" He gave himfelf a ranfom for all ;" the term
is very fignificant, expreffive, and powerful.
All mankind, by reafon of fin, were in a ftate
of bondage and captivity : he ranfomed them, by
giving himfelf in exchange for them : all mankind, by means of tranfgreffion, had rendered
themfelves obnoxious to everlafting punifhment ; but Jefus gave himfelf a ranfom for all,

by taking on him their condition, and expofing
himfelf to all their woes : hence on the ranfom's
being found, they were delivered from going
down into the pit.

If Jefus gave himfelf a ranfom for all, then
are all ranfomed : the prey is taken from the
mighty, and the lawful captives are delivered :
they are ranfomed from the dominion of fin,
from the curfe of the law, and from everlafting
death.   Thus ftands the cafe with all the children of Adam, as ranfomed by Jefus Chrift,
who, in confequence thereof, are fpotlefs before
God.

But this is to be teftified in due time, i. e.
to be made appear or known—which intends,
that there is a time with God called the due
time, when this truth, that all mankind are ranfomed from fin, and from all its confequences,
by Jefus Chrift, fhall be publifhed on the houfe-
top, fhall be made manifeft to all ; not in the

report

report only ; but in the bleſſed, full, and eternal enjoyment thereof.

" Who gave himſelf a ranſom for all, to be
teſtified in due time." O glorious words !
and full of grace and truth ! This is giving, not
only like a King, but like a God : herein is
love indeed. How this grace detects and ex-
poſes the paltry pride of human nature ! The
potſherds of the earth heſitate, yea, refuſe to believe and live upon their Maker's bounty. Their
humility ſays it is *too* good, *too* free, *too* extenſive : their goodneſs complains, that it leaves
no guard againſt ſin : their wiſdom and juſtice
cannot perceive the equity of it ; becauſe, to include *all* is to make no diſtinction between the
evil and the good. But, if Chriſt died for all,
then were all dead. The former is ſo palpable
a truth, as to be taken for granted in the apoſtle's argument · nor does the latter want, but
has the ſame evidence, and is withal undeniably
deducible from the former. Hence, no man
can

can with truth object to the freenefs and extent of the great falvation.

" WHO gave himfelf a ranfom for all, to be
teftified in due time." Here is the diftinction
kept up as before : all are ranfomed, but all
have not yet received the teftimony : does it
follow, that they never will receive the teftimony ? Quite the reverfe. The apoftle fays,
" To be teftified in due time."—Which time
is an appointed time ; it will come, it fhall
come, and will not tarry.

AGAIN, " That he, by the grace of God,
fhould tafte death for every man," Heb. ii. 9.
Here are three particulars to be confidered—
the tafte of death—for whom—by what means.
O death ! who befide the Saviour of mankind,
can defcribe thy tafte ? Who but him can remember, and explain the mifery, the wormwood,
and the gall ? The word *tefted*, here indicates
the fenfe and confcioufnefs which he had of every
ingredient of mifery in death. He became obedient

dient unto death. He made no resistance, but submitted, body and soul, to their proper pains and distresses. In his silent obedience, he tacitly acknowledged his guilt, as made sin for us. He tasted death, implying, that, though there was nothing in the first nor second death, but what he experienced from every sense of speculation and feeling; yet, in point of continuance, it was but a taste: for sometimes the word is taken in *this* sense. The dignity, eminence, and mystery of his person, qualified *him*, respecting, power and equity, to sustain and finish, in a short period, what had tormented the finite creature, with the worm that dieth not, and with the fire which is not quenched; had it fallen on such, it would have been more than a TASTE to them. To Jesus, mighty, glorious, and gracious as he is, it was but a taste; but to us it would have been endless woe.

Jesus tasted death for every man, for all the descendants from Adam : for them, on their behalf—in their stead—and to exempt them

from

from all pains and penalties. Can words be more exprefs ? *For every man*, without diftinc-tion of nation, name, or character: and if he has tafted death for every man, as above, what fhall fruftrate his grace? what fhall prevent their falvation ? Indeed, if righteoufnefs came by the law, the grace of our Lord Jefus Chrift may be fruftrated ; and his tafting death for every man, may have been in-vain: but thanks be to God, righteoufnefs cometh not by the law ; nor hath he obeyed, nor died in vain. Therefore, as he hath tafted death for every man, every man may expect to inherit the joy of his falvation.

IT is by the grace of God, that Jefus hath tafted death for every man : and his grace, in the fcriptures, fits in direct oppofition to all human works and righteoufneffes whatever : hence there can be no reafon affigned, wherefore the moft wretched and worthlefs of mortals fhould not inherit the kingdom of God and of Chrift.

AN-

ANOTHER witnefs, fpeaking of Jefus, fays, " He died not for our fins only, but for the fins of the whole world." Here, the whole world is oppofed to fuch who believe and obey the gofpel : the apoftles and chriftians of that age were the latter; befides whom, all mankind were then lying in the wicked one, and in unbelief : but, left the death of Jefus, refpecting the intent and efficacy thereof, fhould be, by any chriftian, limited to fuch only who believe and obey, the apoftle fays, " He died not for our fins only, but for the fins of the whole world ;" i. e. for the fins of all mankind ; or of all who lay in the wicked one.   Nor is it difficult to determine what the fcriptures mean, by Chrift's dying for the fins of men : they certainly mean, that he indured the pains and penalties due to their fins : in confequence of which, they, the fons of men, are free ; they are delivered from the curfe of the law, by his being made a curfe for them, and are entitled to all the benefits of his falvation : even the every man for whom Chrift died.

I

" UNTIL

" UNTIL the times of the reftitution of all things, which God hath fpoken by the mouth of all his prophets, fince the world began," Acts iii. 21. The times of the reftitution of all things, feem to me to point out the grand and general jubilee, when the fervant fhall be eternally free from his mafter, and the inheritance fhall return to go no more out : but a happy and joyful poffeffion fhall be the portion of all mankind, for whom Jefus tafted death, yea, for whofe fins he died. Reftitution fignifies, to reftore to a primitive ftate, or to bring back to original purity and glory.

" RESTITUTION of all things," i. e. of all things fuffering or fuftaining lofs, by the entrance of fin into the world. Shall mankind be forgotten in thofe times, when all things fhall be reftored! Man, whofe nature Jefus affumed, whofe perfon he fuftained, whofe fafhion he was found in, and for whofe fins he died ! A mother may forget her fucking child, fo as not to have compaffion on the fon of her womb :
but

but God their Saviour will not forget mankind, in the times of the reftitution of all things. But I fhall have occafion to fpeak of this more fully, by divine permiffion, in future letters ; and fhall now pafs on to another fcripture.

" THAT in the difpenfation of the fulnefs of time, he might gather together in one, all things in Chrift ; both which are in heaven, and which are on earth ; even in him," Eph. i. 10. I intend to make ufe of this text, as well as the former, in future letters ; and fhall here but juft take notice, that the gathering of all things into Chrift, muft either imply the gathering of them into his perfon, that they might be included in his life, fufferings, and death, and be entitled to the benefits of his refurrection, according to the promife of gathering the people to the Shiloh : or, of gathering together into one, all the children of God who were fcattered abroad. Or, it muft intend a gathering in fome future period, of all things into the knowledge and enjoyment of Chrift ; even thofe,

who,

who, until that period, are in ignorance, unbelief, and fufpence.

But the former it cannot be, as that redemption is not yet to be waited for : that gathering has been made long fince, and all the promifes relating to it have been fulfilied, and rendered Yea and Amen in Chrift.

It muft neceffarily, therefore, intend the latter : that in fome future period, the times of
which are appointed of God, and at prefent
only known to him ; he will gather all things
in heaven and on earth, (i. e.) either angels and
men, or fuch who in time have believed and
obeyed ; and fuch who have not in time known
the falvation of God, and are therefore, in comparifon of the other, confidered as things on
earth : but here let me conclude this letter,
with affuring you that I am,

Yours, &c.

LETTER VI.

I HAVE fomewhere read in ftory, in what author I cannot at prefent recollect; of a certain tyrant, who had a bed of a peculiar conftruction, on which he laid whom he deemed his enemies, or fuch who unhappily fell under his power; if they were fhorter than the bed, they were ftretched with torture to the fize of it; and if it happened that they were taller, they were lopped to the fize. In like manner, Commentators, in general, treat the facred text: having adopted a tenet, they arbitrarily ftretch, or fhorten the divine word, to bring it to their

fize;

size; of which might be given a thousand instances.

I HAVE no pretension to infallibility, I may
be mistaken: but this I can say, I have no private end to answer, no darling opinion to gratify,
by my hypothesis of a general salvation; and
therefore to be convinced of my error, in this
affair, will not distress my soul. My intention
is, to give the holy scriptures their full scope,
without putting the fetters of tradition upon
them, or trying them at the bar of any man's
holiness, or orthodoxy. This rule I have followed in my thesis, and I hope to do the same
in the antithesis, which I propose to state, and
give impartial attention to.

I AM aware, that much pains has been taken,
and many words have been made use of, to
prove, that the *whole world*, for the sins of which
Christ died, intends only the world of the elect,
or the world of believers; or the world in a
comparative sense: and, that the ALL, by the
same

same chicanery, is suppofed to be not one tenth of the whole. But what is the chaff to the wheat, or human invention to the fimplicity and plainnefs of truth?

There are fundry paffages of fcripture, which men oppofe to the doctrine of God's general love, and falvation of mankind; a few of which I fhall take notice of, and hope, by the influence of that Spirit who firft dictated them, to point out their meaning, in fuch fort, as to give a fatisfactory anfwer to the whole of what may be judged fcriptural objections.

First, " The wicked fhall be turned into hell, and all who forget God," Pfalm ix. 17. " The day cometh that fhall burn as an oven, when the proud, and all who do wickedly, fhall be as ftubble." I reply—Thefe, and all the threatenings, as well as the promifes of the Old Teftament, related wholly to Chrift; and had their final accomplifhment in his appearance and tranfactions. Chrift, made fin for us, fuftained,

tained, as the finner, the pains of hell. "The Lord laid on him the iniquity of us all." "He was numbered among the tranfgreffors, and among the wicked in his death. Thus, in him, the wicked were turned into hell, with all who forget God; in confequence of which, mankind, individually confidered, are delivered from going down to the pit.

WHEN Chrift was made a curfe for us, all the threatenings wherewith the finner and the ungodly are threatened, were executed on them in him : the authority and equity of which tranfaction have their rife, 1. from the will of God; 2. from Chrift's voluntary undertaking; and, 3. from the kindred onenefs fubfifting between him and the people. According to which, through the whole of his obedience and death, He and they were confidered in the eye of juftice, as one perfon : and finners without diftinction, were chaftifed in him. This is what is called in the Old Teftament, " the day of the Lord, a day of darknefs, gloominefs, and of

the

the fhadow of death. The day of Chrift's fufferings, is the day of which the prophet fpake :
the day which fhould buin as an oven, when
all the wicked fhould become ftubble, and the
character of the finner ceafe from man, as pre-
fented unto God in Chrift. For Jefus came as
the refiner's fire, and as the fuller's fope ; that
in the furnace of his affliction, and the wafhing
of his regeneration, he might purify the fons of
Levi: It may be afked, probably, what has
their purification to do with the falvation of all ?
I anfwer—I conceive the tribe of Levi to be
the firft fruit of the tribes of Ifrael : and we
know what the apoftle fays, i. e. " If the firft
fruit be holy, the lump alfo is holy ; and if the
root be holy, the branches alfo are holy." Levi
was to the tribes of Ifrael, what Jefus Chrift is
to all mankind : and, therefore, in confequence
of *his* being the firft fruit, the whole, the lump,
and the branches, of which he is the root, are
holy unto God as Chrift is holy.

K   As

As it is true, that Christ was made a curse
for us, and that all the threatenings issued out
against the sinner and the ungodly, from the
beginning of time, were executed on them as
comprehended and upheld in the person of Jesus : so is it true that all the promises were made
to him, as the seed of Abraham, and that they
are all accomplished and fulfilled in him, and
on the people by him. To this purpose the
apostle, who speaking of man, says, " Thou
madest him a little lower than the angels : thou
crownedst him with glory, and honor, and didst
set him over the works of thy hands. Thou
hast put all things in subjection under him."
This is not only a description of Adam's first
state, but of a promised restoration. " But
now, says the apostle, we see not yet, all things
put under him ;" i. e. we see not yet that man
is thus perfectly restored.—" But says he, we
see Jesus, who was made a little lower than the
angels, for the suffering of death, crowned with
glory and honor, that he, by the grace of God,
                                        should

should taste death for every man," Heb. ii. 7,
8, 9. Hence it appears, that though men, individually confidered, do not yet inherit the
promife ; yet Jefus inherits for them, and unto
him are they to look for the truth of what God
has fpoken. It was in this view, the apoftle
found fatisfaction, when as yet he faw not that
all things were put under him. In brief, I conclude, that all the threatenings and promifes of
the Old Teftament have had their full accomplifhment and perfection in what Chrift has
done, fuffered, and obtained ; and that they
are not to be carried beyond him, or applied to
any matters future to what he perfected on the
crofs ; the revelation and enjoyment of his grace
excepted. Thus, according to my judgment,
there can be no juft objection gathered from
the fcriptures, againft the hypothefis of a general falvation of mankind.

AND, if we only take this obfervation with
us, that fin, in the fcriptures, fuftains perfonal
characters, we fhall find no unfurmountable ob-

jections

jections to this doctrine; nay, not in the New
Teftament: for then that very formidable objection, as it is thought by fundry to be, of the
fheep and the goats, their being feparated at the
laft day, and deftined to different ftates; will
appear to be nothing more than what is meant
by the apoftle, where he fays, " we fhall be
changed in a moment, in the twinkling of an
eye." If fin in the fcriptures is called a man,
an old man, &c. yea, if fin, in a plural fenfe,
intends the many enemies, the armies of the
aliens, &c. as I verily think it does, I perceive
no difficulty in applying it to the goats, and
that the feparation intends the eternal deftruction of all fin and corruption from mankind.
I am aware here of the charge of inconfiftency,
that will be brought againft me. Have you
not (fays an objector) repeatedly afferted, that
our fins were feparated from us, and deftroyed
in the death of Chrift? with what propriety
can you then apply it to matters yet future, fuch
as the feparation of the fheep and the goats,
fpoken of by our Saviour? or how can you
suppofe

suppose a thing done, and yet to be done ? To
the first, I reply, I am not persuaded, that the
separation of the sheep and the goats, spoken
of by our Saviour, is yet future. It was so indeed to the time of our Lord's speaking it ; because he was not then glorified. But why may
it not be supposed, that he was then speaking
of matters to be effected by his decease, which
he was to accomplish at Jerusalem ? I can
easily conceive his cross to be the throne of
his glory ; and that all nations were gathered
there before him, and that he there made the
separation between the sheep and the goats, i. e.
between mankind and their sins, as a shepherd
divideth the sheep from the goats : and that
the character of the sheep there drawn, entitling
them to the joy of their Lord, is none other
than what they have in and by him : or, that
they are not saved by grace, which is contrary
to the positive doctrine of the scriptures : or,
should you refuse this turn given to the parable,
and insist on its relating to a period yet future ;
still it throws no embarrassment in my way, nor

mili-

militates againft the plan of God's general love and falvation of men by Jefus Chrift, provided that the diftinction of fheep and goats be not applied to the *perfons* of mankind, which I fee no reafon for, I confefs.

For, if the goats in the parable intend a part of the human race, they were fuch either from the decree and will of God, or from their own unbelief and difobedience. From the latter it cannot be, becaufe fheep and goats are of different fpecies. It is impoffible for a goat to become a fheep, fuch a metamorphofis has not yet been feen in nature; nor can a fheep become a goat: yet on the above fuppofition, the goat is judged and condemned to endlefs woe, for not converting itfelf into a fheep · and the fheep is praifed, bleffed, and faved, for not becoming a goat. Hence I would propofe, that this diftinction, if applied to the perfons of men, cannot take its rife from themfelves, but the fource muft be looked for elfewhere.

SHALL

SHALL it be imputed to the will of God, that mankind are thus diftinguifhed? Then every man fills up his place, and anfwers the end of his creation. The one is formed for happinefs, and the other for ruin; nor was it poffible for either to avoid his deftiny. This deftroys the diftinction of virtue and vice, and renders cenfure and applaufe irrational. Did God create thofe who are cenfured under the character of the goats to fill up that character? Did he render it impracticable for them to do otherwife; fo that they could not love Chrift, nor his brethren, nor from fuch a principle do them any good office? And muft they yet be cenfured and damned everlaftingly, for being what he made them, and for doing what he appointed them to? Such an idea wear the face of blafphemy in my apprehenfion, and therefore I cannot but abhor it.

OF the like nature is the fuppofition, that the Judge of all the earth fhould publicly approve, applaud, and reward the conduct of thofe under the character of the fheep,

when

when they acted from neceffity, and not from
virtue : for this is undeniably implied, in fup-
pofing fuch a diftinction between mankind,
from the will and purpofe of God.

But, to give the text its full fcope, where the
King fpeaking to the goats, fays, "Depart from
me, ye curfed, into everlafting fire prepared for
the devil and his angels : for I was an hungred,
and ye gave me no meat ; I was thirfty, and ye
gave me no drink ; I was a ftranger, and ye
took me not in ; naked, and ye cloathed me
not : fick and in prifon, and ye vifited me
not."

Here we have the place of their deftination
pointed out, and alfo the reafon of it : Their
place or ftate of deftination, is everlafting fire,
prepared for the devil and his angels. But how
comes it, that thofe goats fhould have what
was prepared for the devil and his angels ?
Does it not feem to intimate, that the difference is only in name ? or has there been any
defect

defect in the foreknowledge of God, that what was prepared for one fpecies of beings *only*, fhould, through accidents unforefeen, fall to the portion of others ? From my early youth (I confefs) I have had many reafonings about the perfon of the devil : I have thought, according to the common received notion of him, that he is either omniprefent, or that there are as many devils as human creatures; or that the devil and fin are one, i. e. the univerfal depravity of human nature, is the devil, whofe angels are the particular corrupt paffions of the heart.

OMNIPRESENCE is an attribute of him who fays, " My glory I will not give to another." Therefore, the devil, or fatan, cannot have omniprefence. How can he then be fuppofed to be prefent with every man, in every nation ? Is not this rather a vulgar idea of him, unfupported by revelation and reafon ? Whether the devils or fallen fpirits are equal in number to the human race, 1 will not pretend to affirm or deny ; on the hypothefis of their being dif-

L   tinct

tinct beings ; from the enmity of the human
heart, againft God and againft his Chrift : for
here the fcriptures are filent. I can with more
boldnefs affirm, that there are angels of glory,
many, yea, innumerable ; and that thefe are
employed as miniftering fpirits, who, by the divine appointment, minifter to the heirs of falvation ; yea, that they learn from thofe unto
whom they minifter, the manifold wifdom of
God.

It is not my intention to deny the perfonality
of the devil, becaufe I believe the perfonality
of that unhappy fpirit ; and, as him, there may
be many more.   But I would obferve, that the
words, devil, angels, &c. are often ufed in the
fcriptures in a figurative fenfe.   Our Saviour
fays to the Jews, " You are of your father the
devil, and the lufts of your Father you will
do :" here, the devil, certainly intends the enmity of the carnal mind ; under the influence
of which they came into life, and the lufts of
which they followed.   And the plural often intends

tends only a greater fulnefs of enmity, and a more powerful combination of corruption.

CONSIDERING the text afore-cited, according to this idea, the devil and his angels, may be underftood of the old man, or the body of fin, head and members : and then the goats are configned over to what was prepared for them-felves, and not for others.

THE reafon of their deftination affigned by the Judge, is truly defcriptive of the nature and properties of fin ; and fuch is the excufe of the condemned, which confifts in a denial of the accufation, and in felf-juftification, i. e. "When faw we thee fo, and did not adminifter to thee ?"

THE fheep were to enter into the joy of their Lord : which intends (as I conceive) that ful-nefs of purity, blifs, and joy, which their Lord obtained through his . obedience unto death, and which he entered into poffeffion of, when received into glory : which joy the *sheep* are to enter into, but not until the goats are feparated from them. May it not be underftood of a removal of fin ? Should the reafon be *literally* applied, it would infallibly indicate, that they are faved by their own works : but *spiritually* applied, where the king reckons to them his own righteoufnefs, and where he confiders *them* as doing what *he* has done ; the words are full of grace and truth : and that they are thus to be underftood, is (as I think) plain from the following obfervations :

First, here is a righteoufnefs afcribed to them as the caufe of their acceptance, which they were not confcious of having wrought in their own perfons—" When faw we thee fo, and adminiftered to thee ?".

Secondly, Here is the union plainly pointed out—" Forafmuch as you did it unto them, you

you did it unto me." An intimation that Chrift and the people are one : We are members one of another, and the body of Chrift in particular.   In that body I ever am,

Yours, &c.

(for Chrift's Sake)

J. R.

L E T T E R VII.

DEAR BRETHREN,

WHAT acceptance my laft letter found among you, I know not; having not heard from you fince (as I fuppofe) it reached your hands : but fufpect it will not be fo acceptable to you, as fome of the foregoing. Some of you will have no notion of fin fuftaining perfonal characters, and may think that my attempt to explain the text is rather chimerical. But, remember, you firft folicited my thoughts on thefe matters, and I give them you as *my thoughts*, and not as an unerring teftimony. If they do not anfwer your expectation, or coincide

with

with your sentiments, I will grant you as
full liberty to reject them, as you do me to write
them.

THERE are many texts of scripture (I confess)
which, in their various figures and images, I
cannot with propriety explain, consistent with
what I conceive to be the truth of the gospel.
But yet this staggers not my mind through unbelief, with respect to the truth ; nor do I from
hence impute inconsistencies to the scriptures.
I always conclude, the defect is in my own understanding ; and indeed I have often proved,
that what has been dark and inexplicable to me
one day, has been light and demonstration to
me another day. Nor does the doctrine of
God's general love to mankind, nor their common salvation in Jesus Christ, depend for their
truth on my explanation of the text. Nay,
should I be mistaken, there are yet other re-
sources, of which this hypothesis may avail
itself in proper place.

" MAR-

" MARVEL not at this, for the hour is coming, in the which all that are in the graves shall hear his voice ; and shall come forth. They that have done good, to the resurrection of life, and they that have done evil, to the resurrection of damnation," John v. 28, 29. Those words intend, either what Christ was about to accomplish on the cross, or what was to be effected by the preaching of the gospel, or the transactions of the last day.

I THINK it is not without some shadow of reason, that I have made this distinction : for it is manifest, that the grave, coming out of the grave, &c. are terms used sometimes in the scriptures in a figurative fense, as Ezek. xxxvii. 12, 13. " I will open your graves, and cause ye to come up out of your graves : and bring you into the land of Israel ; and ye shall know that I am the Lord : when I have opened your graves, O my people, and brought you up out of your graves."

EZEKIEL

EZEKIEL was a prophet to the captivity in Babylonia, who, from their ignorance of the promiſe and power of God, were in a helpleſs and hopeleſs condition ; and therefore, by way of figure, conſidered as in their graves. The text *literally* implies a promiſe of their deliverance and reſtoration to their own land : But, as there is no prophecy of the ſcriptures of a private interpretation, and as they are given unto all for inſtruction and doctrine, I conclude, that the text has alſo a *ſpiritual* meaning, and that it intends the general ſtate of mankind, who by nature are dead in treſpaſſes and ſin ; and therefore repreſented as in their graves. Out of which death, and graves, they are raiſed by the voice of the Son of God, who is the reſurrection and the life : their *perſons* to ſalvation, and their *iniquities* to deſtruction. This was effected when Jeſus ſuſtained both the one and the other in his own body and ſpirit on the croſs In that day, both the people and their iniquities were remembered—the one as righteous and holy in the Beloved—and the other as abhorred, de-

M teſted,

tefted, reprobated, and deftined to deftruction. Thus who had done good, came forth to the refurrection of life ; and who had done evil, to the refurrection of damnation.

THIS is alfo true when applied to the preaching of the gofpel. For then, the voice of the Son of God being heard, they come forth out of their graves ; the people are awakened, and their iniquities with them. The people, the gofpel acquits; by reckoning to them the good that Jefus hath done : but condemns their iniquity to final deftruction. Thus may it be faid, that they who have done good, arife to the refurrection of life ; and they who have done evil, to the refurrection of damnation.

THAT fin fuftains perfonal characters in the fcriptures, is undeniable ; and therefore the above comment on the text cannot be cenfured with a juft propriety: but, as fome may poffibly efteem it fabulous, I fhall explain it in another fenfe ; but not in the leaft contradictory to, nor in-

inconfiftent *with* what I have already faid on the fubject.

Some man will fay—Your comments are unneceffary, why cannot you be fatisfied with the common received fenfe of the text, i. e. that at the refurrection, on the laft day, thofe who have done good, fhall arife to be eternally happy; and who have done evil, fhall arife to be eternally miferable?

My reafons for not receiving this fenfe of the text, are as follow.—Firft, It is contrary to the pofitive exprefs teftimony of the fcriptures, refpecting the means of falvation. The fcriptures affirm, that we are faved by grace, in direct oppofition to all works of righteoufnefs done by us : but to be faved, or damned, according to the good or evil done by us, is to the former a contradiction in terms. Secondly, It is contrary to another plain fcripture doctrine, i. e. that there is none among men who doth good, no not one. There is none good, but one God, &c.

Again, it is contrary to the divine teſtimony—
" That God loved the world—that he will have
all men to be ſaved—that he deſireth not the
death of the ſinner—and that Jeſus died for the
ſins of the whole world—taſted death for every
man—and came into the world to ſave ſinners."
Without reverſing theſe, it is impoſſible to conceive, that our final ſtate is to be determined of
by our own doings, good or evil.

I would therefore, as hinted above, offer
another explication of the text, though it rather
pertains to what I intend in future letters. It
may reſpect that conſciouſneſs with which mankind ariſe at the general reſurrection. We are
told, that there ſhall be a reſurrection of the
juſt, and of the unjuſt. But, that the diſtinction of juſt, and unjuſt, conſiſts of their difference in perſonal virtue ; or in any diſtinguiſh-
ing reſpect ſhewn by the Almighty to the perſons
of the one above the other, does not appear to
me, I confeſs. But, as ſuch who die in the
faith of Chriſt, are conſcious of righteouſneſs
and

and purity in him, and are therefore juft; fo thofe who live and die in unbelief, and ignorance of Chrift, live and die in their fins, and are under the character of the unjuft. Nor is this inconfiftent with Chrift's having taken away their fins. For what the Lamb of God, as a propitiation for our fins, has taken away, and freed us from the curfe of, the confcience of the unbeliever yet retains : hence our Lord's faying, " If ye believe not that I am he, you fhall die in your fins." And thus, at the general refurrection, fome will arife in a perfect confcioufnefs of righteoufnefs and falvation ; and are therefore faid to come forth to the refurrection of life ; while fuch whofe confcience retain their iniquities, will, under that confcioufnefs, arife to the refurrection of damnation. Thus I take the text to mean the different apprehenfions, under which mankind will arife at the laft day : fome in full affurance of a refurrection to life, and others under an apprehenfion of a refurrection to damnation. But it does not follow they muft fuffer what they fear. Let us rather

fup-

suppose, that the age of their sorrows is over, and that the time of their restitution is come. As I purpose to speak more fully of this matter hereafter, let this hint suffice for the present as a comment on the text.

ANOTHER objection is taken from Jude, ver. vii. " Even as Sodom and Gomorrah, and the cities about them in like manner, giving themselves over to fornication, and going after other flesh, are set forth for an example, suffering the vengeance of eternal fire."

THE force of this objection is supposed to rest on the words ' eternal fire', as a proof of eternal torments, and consequently a denial of a general salvation. But let me observe, that the words *eternal, everlasting*, and *for ever*, as used in the scriptures, very often intend only a long time: as I can shew in many instances, if need be; and therefore the word is not always to be measured by the vulgar idea, or the common received opinion of its sense. God promised

that

that he would give unto Abraham, and to his feed, the land of Canaan for an everlafting poffeffion. And again, "I will give it to thee, and to thy feed for ever." We read alfo of everlafting hills, and of perpetual mountains: and of an eternal kingdom promifed to David: nor was it uncommon, for the poets of the Auguftan age, to call their city Eternal Rome: and yet none of thefe intend what the word, taken in a ftrict fenfe, is fuppofed to imply. Nor can it be proved, that the word, as ufed in the text, intends more than a time.

BUT, if this is rejected, I am ready to acknowledge, that the inhabitants of Sodom and Gomorrah did fuffer the vengeance of eternal fire. They fuffered it in the type. The text does not fay, that they are *now* fuffering the vengeance of eternal fire, as vulgarly expreffed. Their fuffering was intended for an example: but there is no propriety in propofing eternal fufferings (when the word is taken in a ftrict fenfe) for an example: for fuch fufferings, as

in

in point of duration are eternal, cannot poſſibly exhibit an example ; becauſe, being endleſs and never finiſhed, the extremities thereof cannot be known.

But, ſuppoſing their ſuffering to be typical, there was an example given : Firſt, of the heinouſneſs of the offence, and then the means of expiation ; i. e. that ſin was to be loſt in its chaſtiſement. To me there appears to be a wide difference between juſtice, and cruelty : Juſtice, in all its decrees and chaſtiſements, has only in view the annihilation of the offence ; and therefore it can inflict the adequate puniſh-ment, conſiſtent with a pitying heart and eye, towards the ſufferer. But the properties of cru-elty are to plague mankind, and to torture the human ſoul : nor has it any other view of the end of chaſtiſement ; it diſtinguiſhes not be-tween the perſon and the offence : and there-fore, inſtead of having an eye, in its chaſtiſe-ment, to the correction and extirpation of the offence, the durable and exquiſite tortures of

the

the offender alone fills its profpect. This is indeed the nature and properties of a *fiend*. But
the *human* heart alfo, fallen, revolted, and de-
praved as it is, is deeply tinctured with it :
hence it is (notwithftanding the interpofition of
a Saviour's blood, and that he bore the chaftifement of our peace) that men are fo attached
to the doctrine of eternal torments.

ETERNAL torments pay no debt. Eternal
torments cancel no offence. Eternal torments
have no fatisfaction to divine juftice. Eternal
torments are inconfiftent with divine purity ;
becaufe fuch a ftate, inftead of extinguifhing,
accumulates offence. Eternal torments are an
abfolute denial of Chrift's dying for our offences, and rifing again for our juftification.

Is it not equally abfurd, to impute the eternal torment of the creature, to the will and
pleafure of the Creator ? This does not confift
with one attribute of the divine nature—not
with juftice: As a man may as juftly be cen-

N   fured

fured and condemned for the colour of his hair, or the features of his countenance, as for doing what he, from the divine appointment, was under an unavoidable neceffity of doing.

Nor is it confiftent with purity: God will not, for his own pleafure, appoint mankind to deftruction, and lay them under the conftraint of iniquity to qualify them for fuch a deftruction.

Nor does fuch a decree confift with the love and mercy of the Almighty: though thefe are what the fcriptures teach, and perfuade men to the belief of, as the means of giving honor to his name. But, having fpoken fomewhat of this in a former letter, I fhall wave the argument here.

Our Saviour, from the dignity and glory of his perfon, was capable of abiding devouring fire, and of dwelling with everlafting burnings. Thefe being the chaftifements of our peace, he

fuf-

sustained them; in consequence of which we are
exempt from penal fire. Of this chastisement,
and of the destruction of sin, and the salvation
of the sinner by means thereof, all the de-
structions under the Old Testament are typical:
such as the destruction of the old world, that of
Sodom and Gomorrah, that of the Egyptians,
the Canaanites, &c.

THESE were all figures (though painful unto thousands) of what was to be accomplished
in Jesus, of the separation which was to be
made in him, between the people and their sins:
and of the full and final destruction of the
latter, through his blood-shedding. This may
account for God's dealing with the nations *now*
in a manner so different from what the Old Testament exhibits.

UNDER the Old Testament, compassion shewn
to their fellow creatures, was a capital offence
in God's chosen people: yea, though it was
extended but to defenceless women, and their

tender

tender infants: a difpenfation without an ingredient of mercy. Its language was, " Tooth
for tooth, and eye for eye ;" yea more, to deftroy and root up who had given them none
offence. I need not tell you, how contrary this
is to the doctrine of our Saviour, who has taught
us to love even our enemies: for this is familiar
to all who read the New Teftament.

If the letter limits the fenfe of the Old Teftament, if the tranfactions thereof were not
figurative and typical, importing good in futurity even to the fufferers, I can perceive no
difference between Jofhua and his Ifraelites in
Canaan, and Cortez and his Spaniards in Ame-
rica. They feem to have had an equal plea for
their invafions, to chaftife the inhabitants for their
idolatry, and to profelyte them to the true religion : or rather put them to the fword, that without moleftation they might poffefs their country.
I have read fomewhere, that many ages after the
deftruction of the Canaanites by Jofhua, there
were pillars or monumental ftones found in
Africa,

Africa, with the following or similar inscriptions on them—" We are they who fled from the face of Joshua the Robber, the son of Nun." If true, it proves, that the ancient inhabitants of Canaan, though heathen, were not savages, or total strangers to humanity and morality; and therefore to be hunted down as wild beasts. Nay, they thought themselves causelessly invaded, and could not but consider their invaders as a banditti of spoilers, robbers, and murderers. So thought the inhabitants of Mexico and Peru, when the cruel Spaniards broke in upon them. What must the Canaanites and Americans think of that God, whose favorites their cruel invaders professed themselves to be, and by whose commission they pretended to act? It was impossible for them to conceive, that he was just and equal in his dealings with them, much less could they persuade themselves that he was love; for love worketh no ill to its neighbour. But the matters of the Old Testament are not to be literally canvassed, and accounted for: they have reason and spirit in them:

them: they were typical, and ordained to teach the Jews the way of salvation by the Meſſiah. Canaan was a figure of the reſt that remained for the people of God. The Canaanites were figures of ſin, and of thoſe enemies of our ſouls, who prevent our entrance into that reſt, until they are deſtroyed. Joſhua was a figure of the Saviour, deſtroying thoſe enemies, and giving us reſt. This is ſupported by the different cha-racters of type and antitype, and the general conſent of the ſcriptures. The type being but the ſhadow of things to come, and not the very ſubſtance of the things, has always its attendant defects; to teach us that we muſt look be-yond, even to the antitype, for the reaſon, per-fection, and ſpirit; and the end of that which is aboliſhed.

HENCE, though the myſtical ſhadow may not, in all particulars, anſwer to what it repreſents, yet this is no denial of its being the ſhadow of ſuch a thing; and indeed, if it did not come ſhort in its efficacy, manner, &c. it would be

no

no longer the fhadow, but the fubftance. To
inftance, Jofhua was appointed to give the people reft; but this was only typical, and did not
amount to the fpirit and perfection of what was
promifed; as appears from the apoftle, who
fays, " If Jofhua had given them reft, then
would God not afterwards have fpoken of another day."

In brief, I conclude, that all the tranfactions
of the Old Teftament were typical, which acquits them of injuftice and cruelty. But they
were all abolifhed in Jefus; unto whofe fufferings and death they all referred mankind, for
the end of their appointment. Since which,
what was not only lawful but inftructive, is
now in the *imitation* unlawful, cruel, and inhu-
man. Thus we may perceive the difference
between what was tranfacted before Chrift, by
the exprefs ordinance of God; and fuch tranfactions as have been fimilar to thefe, fince the
appearing of our Lord Jefus Chrift: the former

er were according to godlineſs, but the latter were cruelty and injuſtice.

BUT ſome man will ſay, Does not this imply a diſtinction, in point of preſent happineſs, at leaſt between the people of former and thoſe of latter ages ? I anſwer—It does, and this the ſcriptures not only ſuppoſe, but affirm in ſundry places ; and ſhew withal, the removal of ſuch a diſtinction by the coming of Chriſt. Until Chriſt, the world were under a typical diſpenſation : the Jews repreſented the church, or mankind perſonally : while the other nations were figurative of their ſins and uncleanneſſes, and therefore were ſubject to typical deſtructions : which deſtructions were all emblematical of the pains of death and of hell, even thoſe which Jeſus endured for the ſalvation of man : and therefore, by way of figure, are ſpoken of as the thing itſelf. Hence, the inhabitants of Sodom, &c. are repreſented as ſuffering the vengeance of eternal fire, while

they

they suffered it only in the type of the sufferings of Jesus; and therefore those visitations,
when threatened, were limited to a certain time.
But I feel I grow tedious, and shall here
conclude this letter, with assuring you that I
am,

Yours, &c.

(for Chrift's Sake)

J. R.

LETTER VIII.

DEAR BRETHREN,

GOD hath declared in his law—That he is a jealous God, vifiting the iniquity of the fathers upon the children, unto the third and fourth generation of them that hate him : but that he will fhew mercy unto thoufands of them that love him, and keep his commandments."

As there are many inftances in the Old Teftament, of the deftruction of nations, cities, tribes, and families, for their fins : fo in all thefe cafes, the iniquities of the fathers were vifited on the children : the children, though helplefs

lefs and innocent, were together with their parents doomed to fuffer death ; the parents *only* being guilty of the tranfgreffion, which brought this common ruin on them. But this does not appear to me to be the fenfe of the text ; I rather think that the iniquity of the fathers, is the fin of Adam ; and that the vifitation of his fin upon his children, intends the typical vifitation ; of which I fpake in my former letter. The continuance of which, until the third and fourth generation, intends until Chrift : who, about the fourth generation from Adam, reckoning to each generation a thoufand years, made his appearance, that all the typical vifitations might meet in his perfon, as the antitype and fubftance of all thofe things ; and in confequence thereof, ceafe from man and beaft. Thus, all thofe vifitations had their final end in Chrift : for in him the iniquities of the fathers being perfectly expiated, and no longer exifting, they could not yet be vifited upon their children.

THIS was the glorious period, prospective in the words of the prophet, where he says, "What mean ye that ye use this proverb concerning the land of Israel, saying, The fathers have eaten sour grapes, and the children's teeth are set on edge? As I live, saith the Lord God, ye shall not have any more to use this proverb in Israel," Ezek. xviii. 2, 3. Again, another prophet says, "In those days they shall say no more, The fathers have eaten sour grapes, and the children's teeth are set on edge," Jer. xxxi. 29. To me it is plain beyond uncertainty, that the time here referred to is the day of Christ: and it strongly corroborates what I have advanced before. It is pretty evident, that this proverb had been used in Israel from the first, and that it was formed from God's declaration in his law :—"that he would visit the iniquities of the fathers upon the children," &c. This declaration is so exactly similar in sense to the proverb, in my judgment, that I can see no reason for retaining the one if we reject the other. Hence there is a particular time mentioned by

the

the prophet, when this proverb fhould ceafe
from Ifrael, becaufe the fource and caufe of it
fhould be dried up, and done away : " And it
fhall come to pafs, like as I have watched over
them, to pluck up, and to break down, and to
throw down, and to deftroy, and to afflict ; fo
will I watch over them to build, and to plant,
faith the Lord," Jer. xxxi. 28. It was on the
accomplifhment of this, that the proverb was
to ceafe from Ifrael. And what does this text
hold forth to us, but our lofs in Adam, and our
recovery in Jefus Chrift ? In Adam we were
plucked up, broken down, thrown down, deftroyed, and afflicted ; fo are we built again
and planted in Chrift, where the vifitation of
the fathers iniquities upon the children hath
ceafed for ever ; and we fhall no more complain, that the fathers have eaten four grapes,
and the children's teeth are fet on edge." In
this falvation, " every one fhall die for his own
iniquity ; every man that eateth the four
grape, his teeth fhall be fet on edge." Equal
to another faying, " The foul that finneth it
fhall

shall die." In him who tasted death for every man: every man has died for his own sins; and every man who hath taken the sour grape, has had his teeth set on edge.

MANKIND were so comprehended in the person of Christ, through all that he did and suffered, that the soul that sinned died, and every man suffered for his own sin. This is a doctrine familiar to an apostolic christian, who can say as the apostle said, " I am crucified with Christ." All this tends to confirm my proposition, that Christ was the third and fourth, or the generation unto whom, and no farther, God would visit the sins of the fathers upon the children. Until then, the people were considered as haters of God : therefore, is it said *of them that hate him.* This is a character, according to the scriptures, applicable to all the children of Adam, considered in themselves : " for all have sinned, and have come short of the glory of God."

THERE-

THEREFORE, the perfect character of loving God, and keeping his commandments, belongs to Jesus Christ our Lord, and to him only : but as we are made the righteousness of God in Christ, as Christ occupied our nature and persons, in all his doings, sufferings, and obtainments, he has cloathed us with his own garment of salvation, and robe of righteousness ; nor is he ashamed to call us brethren. Hence, we are OF him who loved God and kept his commandments, and therefore *we* obtain mercy,

" GOD will shew mercy unto thousands *of* them that love him, and keep his commandments." Will he not shew mercy to *all* that love him and keep his commandments ? Surely he will. If the sons of men are supposed to be the lovers of God, and the keepers of his commandments, intended in the text, why should the divine mercy be limited to *thousands* of them only ? Yea, would not the text then say, he will shew mercy unto ALL who love him, and keep his

com-

commandments? Common sense, I am persuaded,
will adopt the affirmative. This consideration
also contributes its mite to the support of the
doctrine of Christ, i. e. that he is the perfect,
supreme lover of God, and keeper of his commandments; on whose account God sheweth
mercy unto the thousands that are *of* him.

BESIDES, loving God, and keeping his commandments, have a higher claim than mercy:
let the offender, the debtor, and him who has
nothing to pay, implore mercy, and receive forgiveness at the hands of the judge, or creditor:
but loving God, and keeping his commandments, have a higher, a much higher claim.
This character appeals to justice and purity,
and demands divine love, complacency, and delight.

BUT some man will say, If the case be as you
represent it, with what propriety can you make
Christ an object of mercy; since it must be
confessed, that he loved God, and kept his
com-

commandments ? I anfwer, I do not make *Chrift* an object of mercy, but fuch only who are of Chrift ; as his feed, his children, his defcendants ; who, in oppofition to fuch on whom God vifits the iniquity of their fathers, have had the righteoufnefs of *their* Father remembered and rewarded upon them, unto mercy and falvation. They are *of* him as his children. They are *of* him as the fpoil of his crofs, as the travail of his foul, as the purchafe of his blood. They are *of* him as members of his body, of his flefh, and of his bones. Hence, as the fin of Adam was remembered and vifited upon *his* children until Chrift, who took and put away the fin of the world by the facrifice of himfelf : fo now, by Chrift's loving God, and keeping his commandments, God fhews mercy unto thoufands of them that are of him, as faith the apoftle, " But where fin abounded, grace did much more abound.—That as fin reigned unto death, even fo might grace reign through righteoufnefs, unto eternal life, by Jefus Chrift our Lord," Rom. v. 20, 21.

P

I WILL

I WILL not call this a digreſſion, becauſe my aim has been to ſhew, that the divine ſeverity exerciſed on the children of men under the Old Teſtament, whether (by the commandment of God) through the agency of man, or by his own immediate finger, were all typical of that eternal fire, torment, death, and miſery, which, as the juſt puniſhment and allotted wages of ſin, Jeſus Chriſt our Lord had undertaken to endure for the deliverance of the people. And, that it is hence the chaſtiſements and deſtructions of the Old Teſtament are called *everlaſting*, *for ever*, &c. And, that from hence the fire which deſtroyed Sodom and Gomorrah, is called *eternal fire*; and not from its duration, as ſome conceive. Therefore, for any objections that I have yet heard or conceived of, and for reaſons already mentioned, I am ſtill under a neceſſity of thinking, that God loves all mankind—that Chriſt died for all—and that all may poſſibly be finally happy.

BUT,

But, there are other texts of fcripture, which both Calvinifts and Arminians make great ufe of, to limit the falvation of Jefus. The Calvinift will afk me, Whether Chrift does not fay, " I pray not for the world, but for them which thou haft given me," John xvii. 9. I anfwer, I believe Chrift did fay fo: but this faying proves not the error of my hypothefis. Our Saviour, here, is immediately concerned for the perfeverance and fuccefs of his apoftles, from whom he was about to depart; which he knew would fill their hearts with forrow, and whom he forefaw would be expofed to innumerable difficulties, for their teftimonies fake. And, as the fpreading of the gofpel would greatly depend on their ftedfaftnefs, it was necefíary that they fhould be particularly kept: hence he fays, " I pray not for the world, but for them whom thou haft given me:" fignifying, that at that time he had not the world in general, but his difciples particularly in view. Or, that the bleffings which he was then foliciting on behalf of his difciples, were peculiar to

P 2

them :

them ; and were fuch as refpected their manner
of paffing through life.   But the text is no denial of our Lord's praying at other times, for
fuch who were not as yet his difciples ; yea, of
his praying for the whole world ; fo far as refpecting their final falvation.   We are affured,
that he prayed for his murderers ; and that one
who knew the mind of Chrift, thought it right,
that prayers and fupplications fhould be made
for all men.

It was neceffary, for the prefent comfort and
future fupport of his difciples, who were prefent when the Saviour offered up this prayer,
to know how particularly he interefted himfelf
on their behalf ; and hence the peculiarity of
the phrafe.

That his difciples were the perfons intended
in the text, is evident from the defcription
given of them in the context : and that in contradiftinction not only to the world, but to fuch
who might afterwards believe, as appears from

I   the

the words, " I have manifefted thy name unto the men which thou gaveft me out of the
world. Thine they were, and thou gaveft them
me ; and they have kept thy word. Now they
have known that all things whatfoever thou haft
given me, are of thee. For I have given unto
them the words which thou gaveft me ; and
they have received them, and have known
furely that I came out from thee, and they have
believed that thou didft fend me."

THIS defcription of the perfons for whom
our Lord then prayed, fhews very plainly, that
the perfons intended were fuch who were *then*
his difciples. But, as this prevented not his
praying elfewhere, for fuch who fhould believe
on him through their word ; neither did it prevent his ftrong cries, tears, and death, for the
fins of the whole world. If we only diftinguifh
between the apoftles (refpecting the divine interpofition in their favor, and the meafure
which they were poffeffed of) and other men,
yea, even *chriftians* in general, it will appear
that

that the diftinction made ufe of in the text is merely comparative : for in comparifon of the apoftles, mankind, yea, *chriftians* in general, are but as the world, " I pray not for the world," i. e. that all the individuals thereof fhould be thus bleffed, kept, and fupported through life, " but for them which thou haft given me," to be the witneffes of my death and refurrection ; that they may be thus bleffed with efpecial and extraordinary bleffings. In fomething of this manner fhould the text be explained, as I conceive ; and not fo as to exclude the world from the grace of our Lord Jefus Chrift.

BUT the Arminian will yet combat me with another text : Does not Chrift fay, " For if ye believe not that I am he, you fhall die in your fins ?" John viii. 27. There is no purification beyond the grave ; how then can they be faved who die in their fins ? I anfwer, the term being *in fin*, has a twofold fenfe in the fcriptures ; fometimes it intends the ftate of nature

ture (antecedent to our redemption by the blood
of Jesus) wherein the whole world were dead in
trespasses and sin. But from this being in their
sins, Jesus Christ has delivered mankind, by an
equitable and plenary redemption. Hence the
apostle to the Corinthians shews, that the resurrection of Christ is an undeniable proof that
we are not in our sins: his obedience, and death,
perfected and suffered in our nature, name,
and persons, have legally freed us from all
charge of sin: "Who is he that condemneth?
it is Christ that died, yea, rather who is risen
again." From which I gather, that it is impossible for mankind to die in sin unforgiven,
or from which they are not justified by the
blood of Jesus, and innocent in the eye of
God*.

BUT

---

* " Tho' grace may have reversed the condemning sen-
tence, and sealed the sinner's pardon before God; yet it
may have left no transcript of the pardon in the sinner's
breast: The hand writing against him may be cancelled
in the court of heaven, and yet the indictment run on in
the

BUT there is another fenfe, in which the fcriptures fpeak o men, as being, living, and dying in their fins ; and which is the fenfe of the text under confideration. This fenfe implies a continuance in unbelief : for men may, by unbelief, retain and hold faft to their guilt, and fear, and torment, the iniquities which the blood of Jefus hath expiated, and which God hath juftified them from · for a child, an heir, though Lord of all, differs not from a fervant, while in infancy and ignorance; but, having the fame fentiments and feelings, has the fame fervile hopes and fears. Thus his apprehenfion, fenfe, and feeling, gives the lye to the refurrection of Jefus. For, though the latter bears witnefs that we are in our fins, the former pofitively afferts the contrary, and refers us to what is prefent with us.

the court of confcience : fo that a man may be fafe as to his condition ; but in the mean time dark and doubtful as to his apprehenfion ; fecure in his pardon, but miferable in the ignorance of it." Dr. South, vol. 2d. p. 512.

CON-

Conscience, according to some, is repre-
sented as an innate idea, and law of truth, in the
human soul; which, if properly attended to,
will infallibly conduct us to ultimate happiness.
But to this hypothesis, both revelation and
reason forbids me to subscribe. Revelation af-
sures me, that man has, by nature, no light, no
wisdom, knowledge, nor strength, whereby he
should direct his soul into the way of truth.
And reason tells me, that conscience distinguishes
the rational being, and hath its foundation and
rise in the faith and sentiment of the individual.
That mankind are by nature without faith and
sentiment, is not only proveable from the scriptures, but from experience also. I confess it is
difficult to point out the nation so perfectly
savage, that no trace or tradition of the revelation of God is to be found among them : because all have heard, yea, verily, the sound is
gone unto the ends of the earth. Yet it does
not follow, that those glimmerings proceed
from innate principles, or ideas, or from what

is

is vulgarly called natural confcience; nay, the contrary is manifeft. Thefe traditions, though but faintly perceivable among them, are judged to be of a divine origin, only from their having a fuppofed fhadow of confonance to the revelation of God. By the revelation of God, I mean the bible; and this general reference to it is an acknowledgement of its pre-eminence in all things, above every private fpirit.

CONSCIENCE is the judgment of the mind, formed on the faith of certain principles. Whereever a man is perfectly favage, and has no principle, he has no confcience, but is as the brute. Where he has principles, or fentiment, according to thefe, fuch is his confcience. Hence, the difference between the Mahometan, the Jew, and the chriftian, in their divinity, and morality, and in all their dependent hopes, joys, and fears.

NOR has the chriftian man the fame confcience which he always had. To inftance—

when.

when unawakened, and under the influence of education, tradition, and example only, his conscience was as formal as his religion. Conscience, equally indulgent with sentiment, tolerated the sallies of corrupt passion; nor could it record the evil beyond the dictates of sentiment. But when the commandment comes, when the understanding is enlightened, to know the holiness, justice, and goodness of the divine law, we have new sentiments : it is not enough for us here, to have the form of godliness, but we must be possessed of the power thereof. We can perceive no happiness, nor even *safety* for us, short of being perfectly holy, in body, soul, and spirit. These are *now* our sentiments, and *these* give birth and nourishment to a new conscience. This is a delicate and tender creature, so contrary to that which expired with our first sentiments, that it cannot bear the least appearance of unheavenly passion : but, according to the dictates of sentiment, it takes cognizance of, and reproves, not only the evil work

Q 2

and

and word, but the thought alfo, however momentary ; and even the moſt involuntary motion, though hated and deteſted by us. Under this diſpenſation, our principles and ſentiments lead us to ſeek ſalvation, in our own perſonal righteouſneſs and holineſs : but being here continually diſappointed, and convinced, that we are, after all our repentances and reformations, but the unclean thing ; and our righteouſneſſes but as filthy rags. The conſcience conſiſts of ſin, guilt, and fear, and may be termed, an impure and miſerable conſcience, an evil conſcience, &c. Thus the conſcience is always formed upon, and proportioned to the principle and ſentiment of the mind, be it what it may : But when it pleaſes God to reveal his Son in us, as our wiſdom, righteouſneſs, ſanctification, and redemption, we perceive, that all our ſins are expiated and obliterated in *his* blood-ſhedding : and in the purity of *his* life, our righteouſneſs and holineſs are perfected for time and eternity. The truth of which is

verified,

verified, and proved, beyond all controverſy, in *his* glorious reſurrection : in which we are begotten to a lively hope. This gives us another conſcience than we have yet been poſſeſſed of.

But I would ſtill aim at being more explicit, by profeſſing to ſee and believe, that Jeſus Chriſt *perſonated* mankind, through all the particulars of his life, ſufferings, and death ; nor did he fail to repreſent or perſonate them in his triumphant reſurrection. Our obligation to obey the law, in order to life eternal ; our ſins, and penalties due to them, were all made Chriſt's in his doings and ſufferings ; and *his* reſurrection ſtate, in all its ſucceſs, power, and purity, is ours : " he being made ſin for us, that we might be made the righteouſneſs of God in him." Upon this view and faith of the goſpel, the judgment which we form of ourſelves, is according to Chriſt. Has he fulfilled all righteouſneſs ? So have we. Is he juſtified ? So are we.

we. Is he accepted of God ? So are we. Does
he live for ever ? So do we: for he hath said,
" Becaufe I live, ye fhall live alfo :" hence, we
are taught to reckon ourfelves dead *indeed* unto fin, but alive unto God by Jefus Chrift our
Lord.

THIS appearing to us *now* to be the doctrine
of truth, we have a true chriftian confcience ;
a confcience formed upon the principles of
Chrift: a good confcience towards God, by the
refurrection of Jefus Chrift : a confcience that
retains no fin : for the worfhipper once purged,
hath no more confcience of fin ; but is made
perfect, pertaining to the confcience. Thus, refpecting the confcience, a perfon may be faid to
be in his fins, or not in his fins, according as
he believeth on Jefus, or not believeth on him.
And thus I would underftand the text : " If
you believe not that I am he, you fhall die in
your fins." But this has no allufion to the
final ftate of man : for, from the text, it is
mani-

manifeſt, that their being and dying in their
ſins, is wholly owing to their unbelief : but
unbelief is a lye againſt the truth ; the truth is,
that Jeſus is their Saviour, who hath ſaved them
from their ſins : that he is their wiſdom, righteouſneſs, ſanctification, and redemption : but
unbelief influencing the mind to reject the
truth, the conſcience formed on this principle,
retains, in its ſenſe, and guilt, and fear, the
very iniquity which the blood of Jeſus has expiated ; and which God remembers no more.
Unbelief in its term, ſuppoſes a reſiſtance of truth,
yea of revealed truth, yea, of permanent unchangeable truth. For on that moment, the
matter which unbelief oppoſes, ceaſes to anſwer
to the characters of truth ; the oppoſition ceaſeth
to be, unbelief is no longer unbelief : it is no
longer criminal, but praiſe worthy.

To be brief, I conceive a man's dying in his
ſins becauſe he believeth not on Jeſus, to be no
argument againſt all his ſins being propitiated,

re-

remitted, and blotted out before God, through his blood, whom, being ignorant of, he rejecteth. Nay, the contrary is true; and appears, in that the mifery of man is charged to unbelief; which holds faft what God has put away ; and denies the truth of what God, who cannot lye, has declared on his word and oath : hence, in the apprehenfion of unbelief, fin is yet untaken away ; and fuch who die under this influence, die under the fenfe, guilt, and fear, of what Jefus Chrift their Lord, has eternally freed them from the pains and penalties of. Therefore, their diftrefs is not from God by way of chaftifement, or punifhment for fin ; but from themfelves, from their perfonal ignorance, unbelief, and felf-righteoufnefs.

But it does not follow, that becaufe they die in their fins, they fhall never be delivered and brought to the knowledge of the truth ; nay, in future letters I hope to make the

con-

contrary appear, by fhewing that the miferable fhall be reftored to the joy of God's falvation. In this hope I conclude, with affuring you, that I am,

Your fervant,

(for Chrift's Sake)

J. R.

LETTER IX.

DEAR BRETHREN,

AS there are some of you, who are far enough from believing that all mankind will be saved : so are there others, who profess to believe, not only that all men shall be saved, but that death shall administer to them an immediate entrance into glory. To this opinion, I cannot subscribe. Revelation and reason forbid me. The words of our Lord Jesus Christ, particularly noticed in my last letter, make me sensible that men not believing in him may die in their sins : and he has withal declared, that where he is they shall not come.

FOR

For one man to die in his fins, and another not, certainly implies a difference, and fuch a difference, as intends fomewhat more than fuch momentary feelings, as diftinguifh men in the article of death.

Nor indeed are men always diftinguifhed in death, according to propriety of character ; for the wife man often dieth as the fool dieth : the difference, therefore, lies principally in a fubfequent ftate, wherein the one is happy, and the other not.

As you are not unacquainted with the holy fcriptures, you cannot but know, that they abound with paffages which I might quote with juft propriety, to prove that all mankind do not pafs immediately from death to glory ; but thefe, for brevity fake, I omit. To obferve— That Jefus Chrift is our Saviour, and not death. But if death fets men free from their miferies, and adminifters to them an immediate entrance into glory, then death is their Saviour, and not

Jefus

Jesus Christ; then would despair and lunacy be the perfection of faith and wisdom; and suicide be approved of, and applauded.

FOR who would not approve, yea, who *ought* not to approve, of a man's making use of the means which he has in his power to render himself happy?

THIS argument is not only deducible from the hypothesis of all men's being immediately glorified at death; but it is necessarily implied in it: yet the sacred text, which is not only the revelation of God, but the source and guide of true reason, by contradicting the inference, destroys the hypothesis: for saith the apostle, " if a man strive for the masteries, yet is he not crowned, except he strive lawfully," 2 Tim. ii. 5.

THIS text, I confess, has various beautiful constructions, which it would be criminal in me to pass over in silence, though they do not
im-

immediately connect with the thread of my argument, I shall therefore beg leave to make a
few remarks: necessary, as I apprehend, to the
elucidation of the text.

To the prince of the kings of the earth, who
hath in all things the pre-eminence: the lawful strife for the masteries, in the principal and
first sense, relates.

No man that warreth, entangleth himself
with the affairs of this life, that he may please
him who hath chosen him to be a soldier. Jesus
Christ was chosen of God to be that soldier;
and chearfully accepting the office, and engaging
himself to accomplish the warfare, was ordained
and appointed the captain of our salvation.

Jesus, the good soldier, entangled not himself with the affairs of this life. For while the
foxes had holes, and the birds of the air had
nests, the Son of man had not where to lay his
head. He had neither houses, nor lands, nor
money,

money, nor friends, but depended for support upon the equity and justice of him who had chosen him to be a soldier.

A CERTAIN prince noted among his troops a soldier of a sickly and feeble habit of body, who neverthelefs still signalized himself in the fight; courting danger, and defying death under every shape; his courage was confpicuous above his fellows. His prince admired his valour, and determined to recompense it. He commanded his physicians to use their utmost skill for the restoration of his health, without which he was incapable of enjoying riches or honors. They obeyed, and succeeded. But the king observing that soldier (now found and strong) was not so forward and pressing in the battle as formerly, demanded the reason of it: Unto which the soldier replied, Your majesty by restoring me to health, hath made me in love with life, and capable of enjoying it: hence I am not now so lavish of it, as when my want of health rendered life insipid and obnoxious to me.

BUT

But the Captain of our falvation denied himfelf in all things : chofen as a good foldier, to accomplifh the warfare of the helplefs, he entangled not himfelf with the affairs of this life : he neither fought nor received honors of men ; nor did he aim at accumulating riches.

He faid of all who hear the word of God and keep it, " Thefe are my mother, my fifters, and my brethren :" and this he faid to fhew that he was not influenced by partial affection.

Health, property, and paffion (where the faith of Jefus is unknown) are the only fweetners of life. The enjoyment of *thefe* makes death undefirable, while the want of them renders life intolerable. Who is in poffeffion of *thefe*, is frugal of life ; and will preferve it as long as he can : but who is deftitute of them, choofes death rather than life, as the laft refource of the miferable.

The

THE Saviour bare our ficknesses, and carried our forrows, and was all his days on earth, a mourner. Property he had none; nor, as I have hinted before, was he influenced by a partial affection; he was therefore in perfection, that military character which the apoftle drew, as qualified to ftrive for the mafteries.

FROM his kindred relation to the people, the right of redemption was inherent to Jefus, and therefore his ftrife for their recovery was lawful. Again, his ftrife was lawful, from the will of the eternal Father, who chofe him to the office of Redeemer, and invefted him with a rightful claim to the undertaking. Again, he ftrove lawfully, in that he ufed no cunning, fleight, nor craftinefs, while he wreftled, ran and fought for the mafteries; but by dint of pure merit, obtained the victory in all things.

To fuch who know the fcriptures, and the power of God, it is needlefs for me to fay, that

he

he was qualified from his perfect and univerfal
temperance. We are to diftinguifh between the
office-capacity, and the individual, in the perfon of Jefus : according to the former, he
comprehended the people, and their *iniquities* in
himfelf : and they and him being confidered as
one perfon, the chaftifement of their peace was
equitably inflicted on him. But according to
the latter, there was no guile found in his
mouth · he was holy, harmlefs, undefiled, feparate from finners, and higher than the heavens.
Thus qualified for fufferings and conquefts,
no weapon formed againft him could profper,
and every tongue rifing againft him in judgment
he was ordained to condemn.

JESUS ftrove for the mafteries; he ftrove lawfully, and fucceeded. The glorious morning of
his refurrection, exhibited him triumphant over
all oppofition. The law, and fin, and death,
and hell, or what befide difputed the title, or
impeded the path of the finner to eternal life,
lay conquered and flain at his feet. But O !

S   what

what pen of man, or angel's tongue can defcribe the love, the grace, the great good will of the glorious conqueror! When he had trodden down ftrength, and had for ever fubdued all oppofition, he fmiled upon the helplefs fons of men, and faid unto them, "Be of good cheer, I have overcome." When I forget his praife, let me ceafe to exift.

THE ftrife for the mafteries may alfo intend the apoftles and minifters of Jefus, who fhould be free from fuch entanglements of life, as retard their purfuit of the divine commiffion, to preach the gofpel, &c. But, fhould men under thefe characters ftrive for the mafteries, yet are they not crowned, except they ftrive *lawfully*: neither with fuccefs in the end, nor with a divine plaudit in the attempt. The only lawful ftrife *here* is by communion and fellowfhip with the Father, and with his Son Jefus Chrift: By thefe, through the various exigencies of life, they are preferved from all entanglements with its affairs: by thefe they obtain the mafteries,

and

and are crowned : " Hold that faft which thou
haft, that no man take thy crown," faid the
Saviour to the angel of the church of Philadel-
phia.

But where men ftrive according to human
inventions, by rules, orders, and the dictates of
man's wifdom, they ftrive unlawfully ; and notwithftanding their art, labour, and pretended
fuccefs, they are not crowned. Not the defert,
nor the cloifter, nor voluntary celibacy, nor
vows of poverty, warrant a lawful ftrife : nor
will the judges crown who pretend by *thefe or
fuch* means to have obtained the maftery.

The text is alfo explicable to every private
chriftian, who from the firft of his fetting out
in the chriftian religious life, was wholly intent,
by the moft determined ftrife, upon obtaining
the maftery.

Long (perhaps) did he ftrive to deliver his
foul out of the hand of the oppreffor, to extri-

cate

cate himself from ·fin, guilt, and fear, and to obtain righteoufnefs, peace, and joy, in the Holy Ghoft : but neither his fafts, nor prayers, cries, nor tears, would effeſt it ; nay, he could not fo far fucceed, as to be able with confidence to appeal to the judges.

But when the Spirit of truth taught him to gather with Chrift, to run, wreftle, and fight, in the argumentative fpirit and power of the blood-fhedding death and refurreſtion of Jefus ; lo, then he fucceeded ; his ftrife was lawful, he obtained the mafteries, and was crowned by the judges ; even by Mofes and the prophets : " Now the righteoufnefs of God without the law is manifefted, being witneffed by the law and the prophets."

Jesus Chrift our Lord (his free, full, and extenfive falvation) is the only *lawful* method and argument of our ftrife for the mafteries ; againft the law, and fin, and death, and hell,

and

and againſt him who had the power of death, even the devil.

O Jesu's glorious name ! it is full of grace and truth. The law was given by Moſes, but grace and truth came by Jeſus Chriſt : by him came the truth of the ancient promiſe, that all the nations of the earth ſhould be bleſſed in the ſeed of Abraham. For he comprehending mankind univerſally in himſelf, in his active, and paſſive obedience, they were, together with him, entitled to the bleſſings which he obtained.

By Jeſus came alſo the truth of the threatening ; that the ſoul that ſinned ſhould die : for in him, in his humiliation, ſufferings, and death, the ſinful ſons of men were chaſtiſed with an equal chaſtiſement : yea, received at the Lord's hand double for all their ſins. O ! glorious grace, and truth ; they came by Jeſus Chriſt our Lord, and point out to us the lawful ſtrife for the maſteries.

CUR

OUR ftrife *now* to enter in at the ftrait gate,
our ftrife *now* for the mafteries, depends not on
works of righteoufnefs done by us ; but upon
the blood-fhedding of Jefus *alone.* The blood
of Jefus *alone* is our lawful ftrife for the mafteries : by that moft precious blood we triumph
over all oppofition, and are more than con-
querors.

HUMAN nature, being burdened, pants for
deliverance ; and naturally ftrives for the mafteries : fome, to drown the fenfe of their woes,
betake themfelves to riot, or to means of in-
toxication : while others fly for refuge to the
arms of death. But thefe are unlawful ftrifes,
and will cover the victor with fhame and dif-
grace, inftead of glory and honour. He only
ftrives lawfully, who has recourfe to Jefus
Chrift. The blood of Jefus is the true balm
of Gilead, and a fovereign remedy for all human
woes : for of all other means of confolation, it
may properly be faid, miferable comforters are
ye all.

The man who ſtrives for the maſteries, over the diſturbers of his repoſe, over the antagoniſts of his ſoul, by a voluntary death, is not only juſtly reprehenſible for his fear, or pride, or cowardice, but moſt egregiouſly miſtaken in his aims, and diſappointed in his expectations; for the judges will not admit of his being crowned : and he may find to his amazement, that the miſeries which he by unlawful means ſought to avoid, are ſtill upon him ; with this additional reflection : he has *now* by the death of the body, no amuſement to divert his feelings, or thought, for a moment, from the miſeries that ſurround him. The paſſions, which are the origin of human miſery, and which prompt men to ſtrive for the maſteries, by the uſe of unlawful means, are not of the body, but of the mind. It may therefore be conceived, that theſe paſſions attend, and ſway the human being in its ſpiritual ſtate.

May we not ſuppoſe, that Cato was miſtaken in thinking to eſcape the power of Cæſar, by

uſing

ufing the fword againft himfelf. Was he not
compelled to take with him into the world of
fpirits, the paffions which excited him to the
act of felf-murder ? Was he not ftill expofed
to what rendered life fo intolerable ? To me it
appears far from being improbable. It has
more than the appearance of equity and confiftence ; the ftrife was unlawful, he could not
be crowned.

But whether man feeks death, or death feeks
him, yet death is not his faviour ; nor is there
a difpenfation of the gofpel committed to death,
that it fhould preach immediate glory to fuch
who die in their fins, and of whom Jefus fays,
" Where I am, ye fhall not come."

If ALL men pafs immediately from death to
glory, without diftinction ; to what purpofe is
the gofpel preached, and what are the benefits
annexed to the faith of Chrift, efpecially where
men are called upon to fuffer, yea, to lay down
their lives for his name's fake ? To *me* it appears

pears impoffible to point fuch benefits out . if all men, believing and obeying, or not believing or obeying, fhall equally pafs through death immediately to glory. But it is needlefs to combat with multiplied argument, what, without the appearance of reafon, or any plaufible fcripture glofs to fupport it, muft in itfelf appear a manifeft abfurdity.

HERE fomebody, whofe patience is exhaufted, will afk me two or three queftions in a breath —What is the fituation of unbelievers after death ? How are they to be delivered ? When fhall they be delivered ? I reply, the ftate of unbelievers after death is not a ftate of punifh- ment; as this would be a contradiction to the *teftimony* which their unbelief refifted ; and which, from its doubtfulnefs and denial of the faid teftimony, derived its ungodly ex- iftence. The recorded teftimony is, that God hath given to men eternal life in Chrift ; while unbelief confifts in a refiftance and denial of this grace ; blafphemoufly giving the lye to the

T God

God of truth himself. But, if even such who
doubted and disbelieved this testimony, are to
be punished after death, then, the testimony
which they resisted, was not *true* in itself : then
God had not given to them eternal life in his
Son. That this life was not given to them, on
condition of *their* faith and obedience, is evident
from the charge always exhibited against unbelief, i. e. it makes God a lyar : but this it
could no longer do, than the free gift of God
remained : therefore the gift of eternal life in
Jesus Christ, was *to* them and *for* them, when
in disobedience and unbelief : as faith was
reckoned to Abraham for righteousness, even
when in uncircumcision. The gift of eternal
life certainly implies an exemption from condemnation and punishment : and the *permanency*
of that gift, is a proof, that the state of unbelievers after death, is not a state of punishment.

THE state of unbelievers after death cannot
be a state of punishment ; because Jesus Christ,

I

who

who tafted death for every man, bare the chaftifements of their peace ; when the Lord laid
upon him the iniquities of us all : nor does it
confift with the juftice and equity of the Moft
High, to exact from man the debt already paid
by the blood of Jefus ; or to punifh, in the individuals of Adam's offspring, the crimes already cancelled in the facrifice of that Lamb
of God who took away the fin of the world.

But the ftate of unbelievers after death, is a
ftate of unhappinefs and mifery ; arifing folely
from their unbelief : they know not, they believe not, that Jefus hath put away their fins by
the facrifice of himfelf ; and therefore they are
oppreffed with guilt and fear : and *thefe* are in
proportion to their ufe or abufe of knowledge ;
to their receiving or obftinately rejecting the
divine evidences and demonftrations of grace
and falvation ; as our Lord fheweth, where
fpeaking of Capernaum, he fays, " It fhall be
more tolerable for the land of Sodom, in the
day of judgment, than for thee."

THE ſtate of unbelievers after death, is a
ſtate of ſuſpence : oppreſſed with guilt and
fear, they are compaſſed about with doubt-
fulneſs, and uncertainty, reſpecting the final
period.   They dread the approach of what the
ſouls from under the altar cry for.   Have you
any conception of a miſerable man upon earth,
a man without hope, and without God in the
world, in whoſe boſom burns the unquenchable
fire, and on whoſe vitals preys the gnawing
worm ;   a man overwhelmed with guilt and
fear, putting off the gift of God from himſelf,
and though ſuffering the moſt excruciating torment, yet madly daſhing from his lips the *only*,
the *infaliible* healing potion ? Such a man you
will ſay is miſerable indeed.   But whence proceeds his miſery ? It is not that the Lord's
hand is ſhortened, or that there is no balm in
Gilead : Nay, God is good and loving to every
man ; and Chriſt hath taſted death for every
man : and therefore the creature is not miſerable from the want of bowels in the Creator,

nor

nor from any limits fixed by his decrees to the
falvation of Jefus : refpecting its freenefs, fulnefs, or extent. Wherefore did the prodigal
fon attempt, when involved in mifery, to
accommodate himfelf to the diet of fwine ?
was it owing to a lack of bread in his Father's
houfe, or to a contraction of paternal bowels ?
Nay, but to his own pride ; to his oppofition to
his Father's grace ; unwilling to fubmit to his
clemency, and to be dependent on his bounty.
And fuch is the cafe with man : his unhappinefs is owing wholly to his own ignorance,
pride, and unbelief.

Such unhappy people we have known upon
earth, yea, it is a character which I once fuftained myfelf. Therefore, if a man, from
unbelief and its concomitants, may be rendered fo miferable as the above (though beloved of God, and faved in Jefus Chrift, in
whofe blood he hath a perfect redemption, even
the forgivenefs of his fins) fo may an unbeliever

liever be miferable after death, though there
be no chaftifement or punifhment from God
upon him. Hence, I confider the ftate of
fuch, to be a ftate of guilt, fear, and fufpenfe,
proceeding from unbelief: from which they
fhall have deliverance in the difpenfation of
the fulnefs of times.

As to the *means* of their deliverance, I know
no other than Jefus Chrift our Lord : he will
teftify to them in due time, that he gave himfelf a ranfom for all: that he accomplifhed
their warfare, and pardoned their fin. And
when they hear *this*, the voice of the Son of
God, they will live. Then fhall they know,
that the mercy of the Almighty is over all his
works ; and that he hath concluded all in unbelief, that he might have mercy upon all.
For, as their unhappinefs is owing to the
want of that faith and obedience, by which
men believe and fubmit to the righteoufnefs
of God : fo fhall they be infpired with thefe
when

when they hear the voice of the Son of God :
when all with one heart, and one foul, fhall
join in praife to God and to the Lamb, for
ever and ever, Amen.   I am,

Yours, &c.

(for Chrift's fake)

J. R.

LETTER X.

DEAR BRETHREN,

MY letters on this fubject, are drawing towards a conclufion. I intend but this
one ; fhould it therefore be tedious from its
length, or on fome other account, I fhall hope
for your patience.

THE fcriptures fpeak of eternities, or ages,
during which, who died in their fins, were held
in a ftate of fufpence or imprifonment : and im-
pelled by fear, looked only for judgment and
fiery indignation to devour them, as adverfaries
of Jefus. Of thofe ages, and during them, of
the ftate of unbelievers, we find undoubted traces

in

in the volume of the book. An apoſtle tells us,
That Jeſus Chriſt was put to death in the fleſh,
but quickened by the Spirit: by which alſo he
went and preached unto the ſpirits in priſon:
which ſome time were diſobedient, when once
the long-ſuffering of God waited in the days of
Noah, while the ark was a preparing.

Theſe ſpirits were undoubtedly antedilu-
ians, or ſuch who periſhed, and died in their
ſins, in the deluge. They are ſaid to have been
in priſon, when the Saviour was put to death in
the fleſh, but quickened by the Spirit, i. e.
according to conſciouſneſs, they retained their
guilt and fear, and were in dreadful ſuſpenſe,
reſpecting futurity. Such is the ſtate of im-
priſoned ſpirits; their ignorance, unbelief, and
diſobedience being their only chains: In thoſe
chains they lay waiting for the judgment of the
great day, dreading their trial, and apprehenſive
of condemnation.

U,

WHILE

WHILE thus circumſtanced, our Saviour being quickened by the Spirit, went and preached
to them: and that he preached *deliverance* to
them, is not to be doubted. They were under
no other puniſhment, than what conſiſted in
their own ignorance, unbelief, enmity, and diſobedience. And therefore when the Saviour
preached to them, *theſe* muſt neceſſarily fall
before him: while the ſpirits, ſo long enſlaved,
entered *now* into the liberty wherewith he has
made them free. This put a period to that age,
which had continued (with reſpect to the ſtate
of theſe ſeparate ſpirits) from the flood.

So from this æra of ſalvation and grace, to
the cloſe of time, there may probably be another age or eternity; when ſuch who already
are, or who yet *may* be unhappy and miſerable,
as above; ſhall hear the voice of the Son of
God, and live.

THE trumpet's ſound on the day of jubilee,
was typical of this glorious voice; as was the
                                        jubilee

jubilee itſelf, of this wonderful period. It was
the ordinance of the All-wiſe, that when ſeven
times ſeven years were rolled away, the jubilee
ſhould be proclaimed. Various are men's
opinions concerning the ſignification of the
word jubilee; but I join thoſe who think it
comes from the word HOBIL, *to bring*, or call
back, becauſe then every thing was reſtored to
its firſt poſſeſſor. Then was the ſervant free from
his maſter, and the inheritance returned to its
original owner. The ſeventh day was the ſabbath, and (as the apoſtle to the Hebrews ſhews)
a type of the reſt remaining for the people of
God; as which, it was part of the goſpel
preached to the Jews. The ſeventh year was
a ſabbath year, on which they were forbidden
to ſow their field, or to prune their vineyard;
yea, they were not to reap nor gather what
grew of its own accord; but the ſabbath of
the land was to be meat for them all. This alſo implies, *that faith and obedience; in* and *unto*
the righteouſneſs and ſalvation of God in Jeſus
Chriſt; ſo neceſſary to the peace and happineſs

of

of mankind. To ceafe from our own works, neither to fow, nor to prune, nor even to reap, nor to gather, what grew of its own accord, was not a fmall proof of felf-denial and obedience : while to make the fabbath their meat, and to live on the ordinance of God, was a glorious inftance of the faith, which is the fubftance of things hoped for, and the evidence of things not feen ; and which is the caufe and maintenance of gofpel obedience. This is the diftinguifhing character of believers on Jefus. This is the fabbath which thofe who believe enter into, where they ceafe from their own works, as God ceafed from his. But fuch who believe not, enter not into this fabbath, or reft ; but live in the neglect, if not in contempt of the facred ordinance : fuch are they who live and die in their fins.

THERE is yet the jubilee, which in its *extent* of mercy and falvation, ftill far exceeds. Thus who came fhort of the bleffings of the former, were notwithftanding included in the

fal-

falvation of the latter; and, as the elapfe of
feven times feven years ufhered in this glorious
epoch, why fhould we not expect, that the
feven thoufandth year from the world's creation will introduce the grand jubilee? This,
I confefs, is merely an opinion, and what I will
not undertake to affirm, yet I am not alone in
this opinion; for fundry, both Jews and Chriftians, have conjectured, that the world fhould
end in the feven thoufandth year, i. e. two thoufand from the creation to the flood, two thoufand
from the flood to Chrift, and two thoufand from
Chrift to the end. For argument in fupport of
their hypothefis, they refer us to the ufe that is
made of the number feven in the fcriptures,
both before and after Chrift; but efpecially in
the books of Mofes, where feven days produce
one fabbath day, and feven years one fabbatic
year, and feven fabbatic years one jubilee. From
whence it is inferred, that feven thoufand years
will produce the grand jubilee, the clofing fcene
for eternity. Nor, if this laft thoufand years

of

of the feven be confidered as one day (towards
the evening of which may probably be the deliverance of thofe who died in their fins at the
diffolution of matter) will it be unfcriptural?
for in the fcriptures (upon fimilar confiderations
as I take it) we are taught that a thoufand years
are but as one day.

THIS period may be what the apoftle calls,
the difpenfation of the fulnefs of times, when he
will gather in one all things in Chrift, both
which are in heaven, and which are on earth in
him. What fhall I fay to this paffage of facred
writ! It is big wirh heavenly tidings, it is light
in the Lord! and its brightnefs dazzles the eyes
of men and angels—while fuch who diftinguifh
its beauties, and believe its realities, are as men
that dream: their mouths are filled with laughter, and their tongues with finging. Holy and
juft is that reproof wherewith the Almighty reproves the fons of men: " Thou thoughteft
that I was altogether as thyfelf." It is cuftom-
ary among men, yea, it is *natural* to them, to
con-

confider their own frames, difpofitions, feelings, and opinions, as picturefque of facred
Deity.—Hence they aim at fetting bounds to
the goodnefs of God, and to the riches of his
love : to the freenefs, fulnefs, and extent of his
falvation, they conftantly object, ' It is too good
to be true ;' as if the human mind had a ca-
pacity to conceive of goodnefs, beyond the
power, the love, or will of God, to exercife towards his creature ! But to return to the facred
text.

" THE fulnefs of times," certainly refpects
fome period not only future to the æra of the
apoftles, but to that of fcripture utility. " The
fulnefs of times," i. e. when all things reported
of in the fcriptures, fhall receive their final accomplifhment : " The fulnefs of times," according to the myftery of his will, his good
pleafure ; and the purpofe which God hath pur-
pofed in himfelf. The purpofe and will of God
leave no place for contingencies : With the Almighty there is a time fixed for the execution

of

of his will, which neither heights nor depths, nor breadths, nor lengths, nor principalities, nor powers, nor things prefent, nor things to come, may haften or retard. " The fulnefs of times," i. e. the time for the redemption of the purchafed poffeffion ; alluding to the jubilee, when the purchafed poffeffion was redeemed, and reftored to its owner ; according to the ordinance of God. This purchafed poffeffion appears to me, to be that impunity, life, and hap-pinefs, which Jefus has purchafed for mankind ; but which numbers of them, on various ac-counts, have forfeited : having fold them, re-fufed them, difcredited them : fo as having deprived themfelves of the *enjoyment* of thofe bleffings, they are greatly miferable, until the grand jubilee, or the difpenfation of the fulnefs of times ; until the redemption of the purchafed poffeffion, when the poffeffion purchafed by the blood of Jefus for mankind fhall be redeemed out of the hand of the oppreffor, to be enjoyed by the lawful heirs for eternity. ·

For thefe times there is a particular difpenfation referved, which is called, " the difpenfation of the fulnefs of times." Every difpenfation of God to mankind, even from the
beginning, has been with additional evidence of
his love, and grace to them; and with a (ftill)
brighter effulgence of his glorious falvation.
But the difpenfation of gathering together in
one, all things in Chrift, was referved for the
glorious period of the fulnefs of times—until
which period, thofe things were diftinguifhed
and feparate : but *here* they are fought out,
collected, and gathered into Chrift. This gathering into Chrift, refpects *confcioufnefs* only ; for
the gift of God, where he gave us to Chrift ;
to be his fulnefs, and the reafon of his undertakings ; to be the fpirit and falt of his facrifice, and the gathering of all the children of
God into his obedience and death. Thefe, I
fay, were all antecedent to this gathering fpoken of in the text ; therefore the latter muft
refpect *confcience* through the knowledge and
belief of the truth.

X   THE

THE diftinction of things, to be thus gathered into one, as in heaven or on earth, are no denial, in my judgment, to its being intended of mankind *only*, who will at that period be found in heaven, or on earth ; as they wear the image of the heavenly, or the image of the earthly. That the fcriptures fpeak in this manner, is well known ; and thefe would I follow as the more fure word of prophecy. Mankind, as they die in the Lord, or die in their fins, may be confidered as being in the image of the heavenly, or in the image of the earthly ; and confequently things in heaven, or things on earth. Unbelievers are confidered as things on earth ; while fuch who believe *in* and obey the Lord Jefus, as the way, the truth, and the life, are the things in heaven. In the difpenfation of the fulnefs of times, the diftinction hitherto kept up between *thefe* fhall ceafe ; they fhall all be gathered into one, even into Chrift, where the one great falvation fhall be in common to the whole.

As

As I conceive the difpenfation of the fulnefs of times to be yet future, fo do I, that matters inexpreffibly interefting to the fons of men, fhall then be made known to them ; and that the text is to be confidered in that light, as importing falvation, endlefs health, and joy, to all things in heaven and on earth.

THIS " fulnefs of times," the apoftle calls, " the end," fpeaking of which he fays, " Then fhall the Son alfo himfelf be fubject unto him that put all things under him, that God may be all in all." It is extremely difficult, yea, perfectly impoffible, to point out a time, however momentary, when Jefus Chrift was not fubject to the Father, in every fenfe that the term will bear. With what propriety can it then be faid of him, that he fhall become fubject in fome *future* period? Nay, he cannot be the Son intended in the text ; but fome rebellious hoftile, and as yet, unfubdued fon, is there fpoken of, who, when the end cometh, fhall become fubject to the Father. For reafons fuch

as

as thefe, I confefs myfelf totally ignorant of the
Son mentioned in the text, as at prefent not
fubject to the Father, mankind excepted : being aware, that they are in a collective fenfe,
fpoken of in the fcriptures, as the Son, the Son
of God, &c. and, as I take it, the Son not
wholly fubjected to God, even the Father, until the end. But then the prodigal fhall return
to his Father's houfe ; and the Son, in the moft
comprehenfive fenfe, become fubject to the
Father, that God may be all in all.

THIS period is what the apoftle diftinguifhes
with the very fignificant name of *due time* ; when
Chrift's giving himfelf a ranfom for all, fhall be
the teftimony. I have already fpoken of Chrift's
given himfelf a ranfom for all : the teftifica-
tion of which is referved for that period called
due time. Due time refpects the time fixed by
the will of God, wherein he will make known
to thofe who have been hitherto ignorant of
them, the unfearchable riches of Chrift. To
teftify is to witnefs, to certify, to make appear,

or known. What is the fubject? Chrift "gave himfelf a ranfom for all:" And he will bear this teftimony on that day, Jefus Chrift the chief fhepherd and bifhop of fouls. To whom will he teftify his falvation? To *All*, for it belongs to all.   In brief, the text appears to imply, that Jefus Chrift will in fome future period, teftify to all that he gave himfelf a ranfom for them : nor is it poffible, that any teftimony of this grace can be more natural, more convincing,   and forcible,   than that of giving them the perfect and eternal enjoyment of the liberty wherewith he hath made them free.

An apoftle calls this laft, this diftinguifhed and glorious epocha, "the times of the reftitution of all things ;" where fpeaking of Jefus, he fays, " Whom the heavens muft receive until the times of the reftitution of all things," Acts iii. 21.—That the times here fpoken of, were future to that of our Lord's afcenfion into glory, is undeniable (yea) they are reprefented as a

ftate

ftate fubfequent to the finifhed falvation of Jefus, and final : when all things fhall be fo fettled
and fixed as to undergo no further change.
As I pretend to no knowledge of divinity above
what the facred fcriptures teach; Neither do I
believe that thefe have any private interpretation, dependent on the vifionary or acquired
wifdom of man, in contradiftinction to their
analogy and rationality.   Hence it is impoffible
for me to read of the " times of the reftitution
of all things," without conceiving of the happinefs of all things—i. e. the reftitution of all
things to Jefus; which being his by inheritance,
gift and purchafe, are until *then* in great part in
the hand of the enemy.   Hence the pfalmift,
" The Lord faid unto my Lord, fit thou on my
right hand until I make thine enemies thy foot-
ftool"—*Then* fhall death, and hell, and unbelief,
and fear, and guilt, give up whom they have
held in captivity, to Jefus Chrift the head of
all things, as his undoubted inheritance, and the
indifputable purchafe of his blood : when
                                    whatfcever

whatfoever contributed until *now*, to with-hold
their fouls from happinefs, fhall ceafe to exift,
and fear and trouble fhall be no more.

THE reftitution of all things to man, which
are his by Jefus Chrift, and from the enjoyment
of which he may hitherto have been with-held
by the enemies of his peace. Briefly, the reftitution of all things, intends a perfect undoing
of all that fin hath done or caufed ; this it is to
teftify that he gave himfelf a ranfom for all :
In this he fupports the claim of all to eternal
life, on the principles of reftitution : *in* all
things, and *of* all things, made to divine juftice
and purity in his obedience and death.

THE times of the reftitution are undoubtedly
marked in the holy book, in the text which at
prefent is under notice : it is faid of Jefus that
" the heavens muft receive him until the times
of the reftitution of all things :" Hence I conclude, that on that appearance of our Saviour,
which

which the fcriptures teach us yet to look for, this reftitution will take place. Of this appearance of our Saviour, the angels bare witnefs to his difciples at his afcenfion ; " Ye men of Galilee, why ftand ye gazing up into heaven ? This fame Jefus which is taken up from you into heaven, fhall fo come in like manner as ye have feen him go into heaven," Acts i. 11. Of this his coming both our Saviour and his apoftles have often fpoken : and towards the clofe of the facred book we read, " Behold he cometh with clouds; and every eye fhall fee him, and they which pierced him : and all kindreds of the earth fhall wail becaufe of him : even fo, Amen," Rev. i. 7. This appearance of Jefus, is fpoken of by the prophet Daniel ; " Behold one like unto the Son of man, came with the clouds of heaven, and came to the Antient of days, and they brought him near before him : And there was given him dominion and glory, and a kingdom that all people, nations, and languages, fhould ferve him : his do-

minion

minion is an everlaſting dominion, which ſhall
not paſs away, and his kingdom that which
ſhall not be deſtroyed," Dan. vii. 13, 14. Nor
can any thing leſs than the reſtitution of all
things, portend to the full accompliſhment of
that prophecy; where the whole of mankind
are given and ſubdued unto him, to ſerve him;
and his kingdom rendered eternal and unchangeable. Of this his coming ſpeaks our
Lord himſelf, in Matt. xxiv. 30. " And then
ſhall appear the ſign of the Son of man in
heaven : and then ſhall all the tribes of the
earth mourn, and they ſhall ſee the Son of man
coming in the clouds of heaven, with power
and great glory."

I AM here aware of an objection to the hy-
potheſis I aim at eſtabliſhing.—It will be urged,
that this coming of Jeſus is ſo far from por-
tending peace and joy to all, that the contrary
is manifeſt, from its being declared that they
ſhall *mourn* and *wail* becauſe of him, rather

than *rejoice*. I anfwer—Tears are not always marks of mifery and diftrefs; they are fome-times the fruits of joy, and undeniable tefti-monials of inward repofe and delight. And in this fenfe are we to underftand the words of the prophet, " They fhall look upon me whom they have pierced, and they fhall mourn for him, as one 'mourneth for his only Son, and fhall be in bitternefs for him, as one that is in bitternefs for his firft-born," Zech. xii. 10. I have always been influenced to underftand, and view thofe words in a gracious promiffory light; and not as threatenings of mifery and deftruction to the fons of men. They intend the mournings and wailings of faith and love, and are, in the promife, oppofed to that hard-nefs of heart and impenitence, which naturally diftinguifh mankind. This, I think, appears *ftill* more manifeft, when we confider, that this mourning and wailing is not limited to a *num-ber*, as to the non-elect, the unbelieving, the difobedient, &c. but extended to every eye,

to

to all the tribes and kindreds of the earth : which implies *all* mankind, according to my judgment. Therefore thofe wailings cannot be the wailings of deftruction ; for thefe are applied to a number only ; but *thofe* are applied to all without diftinction. The wailings of deftruction are never applied to all, nor are all any where threatened with them. As they therefore manifeftly imply, what all fhall partake of, it is more confiftent with revelation and reafon, and much *more* fo with the love of God, to conclude, that *falvation*, rather than *damnation*, is intended by the wailings of all the tribes of the earth, at the coming of Jefus.

THIS period I confider, as " the times of the reftitution of all things." Then fhall they look unto him whom they have pierced. Under the Old Teftament, the pafchal lamb was ordained to be flain by the whole affembly of the congregation ; as a figure of Jefus being pierced

by

by all mankind. For (the reason and intent of his death understood) it appears that all the children of Adam, both Jew and Gentile, were accessaries to his death; in that he died for all The iniquities of us all were laid upon him, and he was wounded for our transgressions, and his soul was offered for our sins: yea, saith the apostle, "for the sins of the whole world." And as those, who by their iniquities caused his death, with all its shame and torment, may with propriety be termed his crucifiers, so may they be said to have pierced him. To look on him whom they have pierced, implies more than contrition, arising from such a conscious view: for the end and design of his sufferings considered as bearing our iniquities, to exculpate our persons: It appears, that as from the contact subsisting between him and us, in the article of his death, we may be said to have pierced him; so our piercing him, in this sense, interests us in all the benefits arising from his blood-shedding and death: therefore, to look

3   on

on him whom they have pierced, implies an appropriation of thefe benefits : a confcioufnefs of his dying for our fins, in confequence of which, we are juftified in him. Hence, if every eye fhall fee him, if all fhall look upon him whom they have pierced, then fhall all on that day be confcious of falvation and happinefs in him ; and the time of his glorious appearance prove " the times of the reftitution of all things :" when to him the Son of man fhall be given dominion, and glory, and a kingdom —that all people, nations, and languages, fhall ferve him : his dominion is an everlafting dominion, which fhall not pafs away, and his kingdom that which fhall not be deftroyed.

The fcriptures fpeak of things, fometimes as they are with God, and at other times, as the ignorance, unbelief, and fears of man reprefent them ; hence, that difference and feeming contradiction, with which they are taxed by unbelieving critics. I have already hinted, that

where

where they fpeak of the refurrection of the
juft, and of the unjuft ; and of fome arifing to
the refurrection of life, and others to the refurrection of damnation ; they refpect the different
confcioufnefs under which mankind are in their
death, and at their refurrection : and their different views and apprehenfions in their rifing,
to the general appearance on that folemn day.
The one arifes, confcious of righteoufnefs, and
in full affurance of eternal life. But the other,
confcious of fin and guilt, arifes in dreadful
fufpenfe, looking for judgment, and fiery indignation. But it does not follow, that they
ftand *thus* diftinguifhed in the eye and purpofe
of God ; who having loved mankind, and
given them grace in Chrift, he beholds them
only in that grace and perfon. Both you and
I have known at one time or other, the re-
prefentations of unbelief and guilty fear, to be
the perfect reverfe of things as they are with
God : and which, at fome period future to
that of our diftrefs, we knew to be fo. But
while

while under the deception, what miseries did we not feel? What terrors are there, which did not then invade our bosoms? what dreadful apprehensions, that did not then disturb our repose? Nor had we any other means of deliverance than Jesus Christ, revealed, known, and believed on. But when favoured with this grace, when made acquainted with the salvation of Jesus, we could plainly perceive, that our former terrors were altogether groundless; being simply the effects of ignorance and unbelief.

For days, or months, yea, possibly for years, we were tormented with the guilty creations of distempered fancy; the terrifying coinage of an affrighted imagination. But yet, though the cause was fictitious, the effects were real; we were indeed unhappy, and the miseries which we professed to feel, were unfeigned.

Why may not this be the case with others for a longer period; since, before the Eternal, a thou-

a thoufand years are but as one day ? We
have feen amongft men, who, from the fame
caufe, have been all their life fubject to bondage, and to the fear of death ; and yet, at
their laft hour, have been given to underftand, that they had no caufe of fear, from
any limitations in the love of God: no caufe
from any deficiency in the falvation of Jefus,
to afflict their fouls for a moment : but, that
in the times of their foreft diftrefs, their title
was good, and their claim indifputable to the
joy of their Lord.

THE cafe is exactly parallel with fuch who
die in their fins, and continue in that miferable
fufpence fpoken of before, until " the times
of the reftitution of all things."

THUS, according to your defire, you have
my thoughts, without referve, on the freenefs, fulnefs, and extent of the great falvation. Was I aware of any difhonour to Jefus

fus Chrift our Lord, from the publication of thefe letters; of their being injurious to fociety, or hurtful to individuals, I would take care that they fhould not extend beyond your perufal.

But, as the *contrary* appears to me to be true ; confcious of the uprightnefs of my motives, I am content they fhould be printed and publifhed : in order to which (having attentively read them) I defire you would return them to me, as I have kept no copy thereof.

If it fhall pleafe God, our Saviour, to blefs what I have written, to the inftruction and confolation, though but of a few among men, I fhall have the reward I feek, and what will abundantly recompenfe me for all the reproaches unto which thefe letters may poffibly fubject me.

Z   Bre-

BRETHREN, farewel, take me with you into the Holiest, nor ever forget me before the throne of God and the Lamb, *in* whom, and *for* whose sake, I am,

Your Brother and Servant,

J. R.

LET.

LETTER XI.

DEAR BRETHREN,

TO finish, with my laft letter, our corref-
pondence on the fubject of a general falvation, and all its relatives, was my fincere
intention: but, as you now afk me, What manner of perfons they ought to be who believe
thefe things? and folicit an anfwer; I feel my
pen inclined to comply with your defire, though
aware of the difficulty of the undertaking.

BETWEEN felf-righteoufnefs and profanenefs,
the path is narrow; fo that there are but few

who

who find it: and fewer ftill, who with an upright perfeverance walk therein.

THE defcription of this path, and of the
walk of the upright therein, will, as I conceive,
contain a full anfwer to your letter ; and in particular a folution of your leading queftion : by
fhewing what manner of perfons the worfhippers
of Jefus ought to be, and in reality are, while
they fupport that character.

A DETERMINED foul, and a firm ftep are
neceffary ; or men totter, ftagger, flide, and fall
from the terra firma of the gofpel, into the
fwamps and mires of felf-righteoufnefs on the
one hand, or down the rocky precipice of profanenefs on the other.

THERE is a petition in the Pfalms, which I
can never fufficiently admire : thefe many years
my foul hath adopted the words (as I believe) in
their reafon and fpirit : and in all her afpirations
and prayers to God her Saviour, makes not only
a con-

a conftant, but a neceffary and gofpel ufe of them : " Reftore to me the joy of thy falvation, and uphold me with thy free Spirit."

In words, I confefs my poverty ; to fay what I *conceive* and *feel* in the ufe of this petition : How very poor, then, my explanatory attempts, compared with the gofpel majefty and ultimate fenfe of the facred text ! but yet fuffer me to contribute my mite.

On reading this, who are converfant with my writings, will naturally recur to my glance on the fubject, in a former publication : I am aware of it, I confefs it : the propriety, beauty, and fenfe of the words, compel me to repetitions, and to difregard the imputation of tautology.

By the joy of God's falvation, I mean what the defpairing mariner feels, when floating on a plank, in the midft of a wide tempeftuous ocean, tormented with hunger and thirft, and

expiring

expiring through fatigue : He is unexpectedly taken up by a ship providentially directed into that path.

By the joy of God's salvation, I understand what the condemned criminal feels, when dragged up from his cell, on the morning appointed for him, to receive the wages of his iniquity : he is surprized with a free and full pardon.

But what are these when compared with the spiritual and eternal! By the joy of God my Saviour's salvation, I mean, what that man feels, upon whose vitals the never-dying worm has preyed; in whose bosom the quenchless flame was kindled ; when the blood of sprinkling sets him free.

Oh ! what is then his joy ! who can describe it ? He is as a man who dreams, his heart is filled with laughter, and his tongue with singing. Freed from doubt, from guilt, from fear ; and

as the lily of the field, fo arrayed, that Solomon
in all his glory could not compare with him : his
joy is great ; it is joy infinitely furpaffing,
what the increafe of corn, and wine, and oil,
produces.

In many hearts this joy rufhes with impetuous
torrent ; regardlefs of prudential bounds, it
fweeps all before it : Thought, reafon, argument, are fo deluged, that we can have no recourfe to either ; but for a feafon paffively float
upon the fwelling tide.

We read of the difciples of Jefus, that they
wondered, and believed not for joy : this was
the joy of his falvation, infinitely furpaffing
their hope and expectation. That *fear, forrow,
diftrefs,* fhould impede our faith, and prevent our
believing, is not at all furprizing : but that joy
fhould do it ; joy, arifing from the manifeftation
of the wifhed for, longed for, defired object ;
is what fome have experienced, but what few
can account for.

Hope

HOPE and fear mingle in every defire of the human heart; the compound is neceffary to form and fupport a proper balance : for we fink as lead, or mount as a feather, in proportion to the impulfe and prevalence of thefe paffions.

WHEN fear predominates, and drags the foul down to bondage ; hope ftruggles for her deliverance, and refcues her from defpair. Again, when hope is elevated with profpect, and all her foul on tiptoe ; fear infinuates it may be a deception ; it is beyond a rational, and too *too* great a felicity to be true.

THE juftle of hope and fear, renders joy tumultuous, and for a time prevents the mind deciding the grand queftion, Is IT TRUE ? Revelation, the parent of hope, is in the affirmative, and perfuades men ; but the mifgiving human heart, foolifh and flow to believe, the origin of fear, is on the other fide of the queftion ; and fays, it is too good to be true ; yea it fays it, of what amounts to the plaineft demonftration.

THE

THE joy of his falvation, intends that happy ftate, where the tumult is over, and perfect love and peace have taken place. Where reafon and fpirit walk hand in hand, and the way of God with man is juftified. "Reftore to me the joy of thy falvation," is a petition not limited to the cry of a foul in diftrefs, as having loft the Comforter, and begging the reftoration of what it was once poffeffed of ; but it extends to the prayer and demand of faith. That joy, which thou, my Lord, my forerunner, and captain of my falvation, haft obtained through obedience and the fuffering of death : The joy which was fet before thee, when thou enduredft the crofs and defpifedft the fhame ; that joy I claim as my property : I had loft it, but thou haft recovered it, reftore it unto me : for thou art faithful and true. It is mine from thine own declaration ; for thou haft faid, "The glory which thou haft given me, I have given them." The joy of thy falvation is mine, from the reafon and fpirit of thy undertaking : from thy kindred relation to me, the right of my redemption was thine :

from thy being found in fafhion as a man, thou hadft the capability of humiliation to death, yea, even to the death of the crofs. In my name, nature, and perfon, thou engageft thine heart, to draw near unto God: thou haft fulfilled all righteoufnefs, thou haft trodden down ftrength: thou haft vanquifhed fin, and death, and hell, and haft called upon and required helplefs man to be of good chear; inafmuch as thou haft overcome the world; and again, directing thy fpeech to us, " This is the victory that overcometh the world, even your faith. Reftore unto me therefore the joy of thy falvation, and uphold me with thy free Spirit."

THE joy of God our Saviour's falvation, renders all his ways, ways of pleafantnefs, and all his paths peace. What is the profeffed worfhipper of Jefus, without this joy? A mere formalift, who preaches from felfifh motives, who hears the word preached, reads, prays, and converfes on divine fubjects, from fentiment deftitute of affection: either acting from duty, as a flave

who

who dreads the whip, or, as perfons under particular diforders of the body, who, when refo-
lute to be active, are obliged to offer violence to
their feelings. For, in fuch cafes, the leaft
movement feels irkfome, yea, unnatural ; and
is not atchieved without a fentimental refolution ;
and even then exercife is unpleafurable. The
door grates upon its hinges, and the wheel drags
upon its axle-tree for want of the oil of joy.

But where the joy of his falvation is, the
name Jesus is as ointments poured forth : yea,
becaufe of the favour of his good ointments,
the virgins love him. Then it is known that
his fervice is perfect freedom, and his fabbath a
delight. Such manner of perfons the worfhippers of Jefus *ought to be*, and in reality *are*,
while they fupport that character, by walking in
the light, as he is in the light.

But, though the joy of his falvation be fo
neceffary to the confolation of the fons of God,
yet the enjoyment is not without a careful and

cautious

cautious watch kept up in the foul; left our
feelings fhould engage our attention, and divert
the eye from Jefus. Thus, where we petition
for the joy of his falvation, it immediately follows, " and uphold me with thy free Spirit."
That Spirit which requires nothing of me, in order to my perfeverance in the joy of thy falvation. For, taught by experience, I know I
can *do* nothing, I feel I *am* nothing; unequal to
the eafieft conditions, I pray to be upheld by thy
free Spirit. That Spirit, the Comforter, who
fpeaketh not of himfelf, of his own work, opera-
tions, impulfes, and reformations, influencing us
to gather with thefe : but inceffantly glorifies
Jefus, who by receiving of the things that are
his, and fhewing them unto us, invariably in-
ftructs and inclines us to gather with him.

" UPHOLD me with thy *free Spirit*," that Spirit who, while he cultivates and prepares the
mind for the reception of truth, and pours the
oil of joy, even the joy of thy falvation, abundantly into the foul; yet, with pointed finger
                                        and

and irrefiftible perfuafion, converts all our attention to the crofs : There, fays he, is the Beloved, there is your God, your Saviour, your
hufband, your brother, your friend : he is your
wifdom, your righteoufnefs, your fanctification,
and redemption: O! he is your All in All.
Let even your eye towards him be the eye of
the chafte virgin.

O God my Saviour, though I am fenfible that
the joy of thy falvation is abfolutely neceffary to
my comfort, and happinefs through life, and in
thy worfhip, and therefore cannot but pray for
it : yet fuffer me not to be in bondage to the
moft fpiritual enjoyment ; let no pleafing frame,
nor feeling of my foul, however heavenly it may
be, take place of thy perfon, nor ever permit the
joy of thy falvation to rival thy falvation itfelf.
" Therefore, uphold me with thy free Spirit."

It may poffibly be objected, that fuch diftinctions are needlefs niceties.—I reply, Real
chriftianity hath its delicacies, which none are

aware

aware of, but such who know the scriptures and the power of God. I mean to apply them to such only who believe what is contained in the former letters: and concerning whom you enquire, where you ask me, " What manner of persons they ought to be who believe those things?"

I am sensible that I am not yet in your path; you had in your enquiry, an eye to demeanor and conduct, while I have been speaking of somewhat seemingly foreign to the subject. But, before I begin to build, permit me to lay the foundation, and in excuse of my manner, to tell you—that that man's conduct can never be right, whose heart is wrong.

Contrary to the common received opinion, I averr, that in proportion as men recede from the virtue and glory of the gospel, and become guilty slaves to their passions, they grow legal and self-righteous.

On

ON the other hand, profaneness and irreligion, in such who may be supposed to have once known the truth, take their rise from wisdom, faith and holiness in their own conceit. When you read this, possibly you may censure it, as an odd conceit of mine. I confess it wears such an appearance, yet it consists with truth, as I shall have occasion to shew.

THE christian conscience, I am persuaded, will vouch for the truth of what I say : for says the christian, while I walked in the light, I loved my brother, and saw none occasion of offence or stumbling in him : I measured to him, the same measure as I did to myself; i. e. the free and full salvation of Jesus, without works of of righteousness, as done by man. While I walked in the virtue and glory of the gospel, unto which Jesus hath called us, by his life, death, and resurrection, all was light, love, liberty, and heavenly mindedness. But when by means of some irregular appetite, the gratification of some lust, or passion, not looking to

I

Jesus,

Jesus, the author and finisher of our faith;
guilt has been incurred, the scene has immediately changed ; the glorious vision vanishes :
Moses is read, the veil is upon the heart : the
love, grace, and lenient genius of the gospel,
have no longer their charms ; but are despised,
and forsaken, for the austerity, rigor, and censure of the law.

Here the mind undergoes a change equal to a
figure used by an apostle, " The dog returns
to his vomit, and the sow that was washed to
her wallowing in the mire."

Under the sense of guilt, compared by the lip
of truth, to the gnawing worm ; it is natural for
man to fly to his own repentances, prayers, and reformations, for the redress of present grievances,
and for the reason and ground of his future expectations : instead of applying to the Lamb
of God, who taketh away the sin of the world,
and to his precious blood, which cleanseth from
all sin. The mind and conscience being defiled,

men

men lofe their *relifh* for the grace of our Lord
Jefus Chrift, and grow doubtful of its virtues,
and by degrees of the authenticity of the gofpel.

WHEN I perceive the man, who once believed
and rejoiced in the free falvation of Jefus, turn
again to the law in fearch of perfection ; and
from extolling the perfon, life and death of the
Saviour, as the fole fource of his prefent happinefs, and the only foundation of his future hope
and expectation ; I fay, when I perceive fuch a
one fet up a talker for his own righteoufnefs,
boifteroufly avowing, or flily infinuating the
utility, yea, the *neceffity* of humiliations, prayers,
tears, reformations, attachment to ordinances,
&c. growing devoutly auftere, and pioufly cen-
forious ; I repeat, when I meet with fuch a
character (which I often do) the words of the
apoftle ftill recur, " The dog to his vomit, and
the fow that was wafhed to her wallowing in
the mire." I am perfuaded, that this character
originates from the diftrefs of unbelief, and is
the genuine offspring of a wounded confcience.

B b.   CHRIST

CHRIST and Belial cannot dwell together, nor can guilt and the gospel inhabit the same soul: where the gospel is entertained, guilt can find no place. But where the gospel is hid, or, losing its spiritual demonstration and power, dwindles into word *only*—there guilt obtains : men think with that Syrian, who scoffingly asked, If the rivers of Damascus were not preferable to the waters of Jordan ?

IN looking around me, I have observed among mankind, that it is thought sufficient to *patronize* virtue and purity, without entering into the spirit and practice thereof. A pious reflection, a compunctive sigh, with a prayer in the evening, atones for the evil of the day, and hushes the worm to sleep, under the notion of its being a child of grace. There are a few particulars in *their* catalogue of vices, which, if in the most favorable selfish partial construction, they chance to escape, they fail not to number themselves among the saints, and to look down upon their brethren.

THE

THE free gospel which preaches salvation to helpless man, without works of righteousness done by him, is commonly accused of libertinism. But let me tell you, the law and human righteousness, have their libertines also : witness the religious disputes of the day, as well as of ages past.

THE greatest patrons of human holiness, yea, even the bold angelic assertors of personal perfection, are wise in their generation, as the children of this world : There is no cunning sleight, or craftiness, that they will not avail themselves of, to give their adversary the fall ; though they can consistently promise nothing to the public by it, nor to themselves, except a little pelf, and the whistling of a name : for whom they pretend to overthrow, they confess to be their fellow saints and servants of Jesus. They also hold up to the public, in the character of the reprobate, persons whom they never conversed with, nor even knew by face ; and in defence of their conduct, appeal to the world for the truth of their infinuations : chearfully admitting the accuſer of the brethren himſelf, an evidence againſt them.

THIS is a picture in miniature, of a ſelf-righ-teous, ſelf-holy libertine, a vile tranſgreſſor, both of the law of Moſes and of Chriſt.

To do evil that good may come, is a maxim exploded with abhorrence by the apoſtle, as in-compatible with chriſtianity, and an abomination before God and our Saviour ; yet this abomi-nation is practiſed, even in the high places of the ſelf-righteous, and lies mingled with their offerings upon the altar.

THAT men bite and devour one another, is certainly an evil : that they whiſper, mutter, backbite, and flander, is evil : that they miſre-preſent, and uncover each others nakedneſs be-fore the face of the ſun, is undoubtedly an evil : but theſe and a thouſand more of like nature, are eaſily accounted for, eaſily anſwered, and

the

the ſtain wiped out, with this ſingle plea, " Our aim is to do good."

WHOM ſelf-righteous men mean to traduce, they make public prayer for : and when from rigid virtue, awful juſtice, or an affected ſimplicity of piety, they find it indiſpenſible to tell God Almighty the crimes or infirmities of the culprit, they are extremely circumſtantial, except it ſuit their purpoſe better, and the policy of the cauſe requires, that they ſhould pretend to a rod in reſerve ; which, but for their lenity, would chaſtiſe the offender as with ſcorpions : here a ſomething inſinuated to be highly culpable, muſt be nameleſs.

SOMETIMES the accuſation relates to matters of faith, and ſometimes to manners : but error in matters of faith, the public are inclined to wink at. Therefore hereſy without the ſauce of corrupt manners, is but an inſipid diſh in theſe days : add but the ſauce with a high ſeaſoning, the prieſt and the peaſant will feed with delight :

light: " They eat up the fins of my people," fays the prophet.

YEA, fay you, but this relates to priefts of the Roman perfuafion, who derive advantages of riches and power, from the fins of the people. But I averr, it is true alfo of who call themfelves Proteftants, and particularly applicable to the greateft pretenders to holinefs among them.

AMONGST thefe, the foibles and infirmities of one man *feeds*, yea, *fattens* another : either as they reap confolation from comparifon, or by thefe fteps afcend to fuperiority. I have heard it reported of the holy author of the Saints everlafting Reft, that he had an inclination even to longing, to ferve up Dr. Crifp to himfelf, and the public, as a heretical difh of the firft relifh : but to his great mortification, he found, after the moft critical enquiry, that he could not with all his art, procure a proper fauce ; without which the difh would be unpalatable to much the greater part

of

of mankind: Hence, the pious complaint,
That, but for Dr. Crifp's purity of manners,
they could eafily have refuted his doctrine, and
have held it up in fuch a light to the public,
as would diveft it even of the appearance of
truth, and its author of credit.

O! felf-righteoufnefs, what a Proteus art
thou! Nothing can be more frequent in the
mouths of thofe gentry, than that, " That
man's faith can never be wrong, whofe life is
right." Yet they mean this only to Arminians,
Arians, Socinians, Deifts, Jews and Heathen.
Among thofe, whofe life is fuppofed to be upright, they entitle to the love and favor of God;
however difconfonant their faith may be to the
facred fcriptures, yea, though they ftand charged
in the latter, with having no faith at all: " For
all men have not faith."

But (fay you) do they not mean to apply it,
as well to fuch who are on the other fide of the
queftion? nay, far, very far, are they from applying

plying it to a true difciple of Jefus : however
unqueftionable the uprightnefs of *his* life may
be, yet its evidence for the truth of *his* faith,
fhall not be admitted : nor its recommendation
in the leaft attended to ; as I have obferved in
in the cafe of Dr. Crifp : and I may here add,
in the cafe of the apoftle Paul himfelf : Paul, did
I fay ! let me ftill add, in the cafe of one greater
than Paul, who fays, " Which of you convinceth
me of fin, and if I fpeak the truth, why do you
not believe me ?"

You will naturally afk, whence this bias, this
abfurd partiality, fo palpable and glaring? It
originates from nature, by which man is a child
of wrath, without hope, and without God in the
world : the child of wrath, does not imply an
objeƈt of the divine anger, or fury, refpeƈting
the perfons of men, as fundry dream ; but relates to that enmity, and wrath againft God, and
againft his holy child Jefus, wherewith fatan im-
pregnated the human heart, when he fowed the
evil feed ; of which the Saviour fpake, where he
                                    fays,

fays, " Ye are of your Father the devil, and the
lufts of your Father ye will do." Thefe lufts
confift in enmity to Jefus Chrift, in particular to
his free, full, and extended falvation of mankind, without works of righteoufnefs as done
by them. Naturally, we know nothing of this
grace, we have no idea of it, and when we begin
to hear and enquire, the father of ignorance and
unbelief accufes it of deception, irrationality,
and impofture ; that it is deftructive to virtue,
goodnefs, and holinefs.

Nor need they, who are by nature and bias
children of wrath, and [the feed of the ferpent,
much perfuafion on this head : the prince of
this world, when he cometh, ftill finds fomewhat
in them. Such is the bias under which every
human heart is born into this world, and therefore we are all children of wrath, by nature :
Ignorance, doubtfulnefs, unbelief, and enmity
to Chrift and to his great falvation, conftitute
the intellectual feeling, and acting character of
every child of Adam, while in the ftate of na-

ture,

ture; without hope, and without God in the world. Nor (when every thought is brought into captivity to the obedience of Chrift) are we perfectly exempt from the affaults of felf-righteoufnefs; for, though felf-righteoufnefs may be no longer predominant, or the principle that fways the foul; yet it inheres in the human heart, an evil feed, which, however diligently and carefully weeded, is not perfectly eradicated while we are in the body, "This vile body muft be changed."

Where felf-righteoufnefs is allowed of, and every virtue and glory, and even falvation itfelf, are placed to that account; it is by way of compenfation for fin to expiate accumulated guilt, and to palliate infirmity. " Without holinefs no man fhall fee the Lord." Holinefs is abfolutely neceffary to our confolation, and to our confidence towards God. For, if our hearts condemn us, we have no confidence towards him. This neceffary holinefs, men gather with divers means, and from different quarters. The chri-

ftian

ſtian *indeed* gathers with Chriſt, who of God is
made unto us ſanctification : Conſcious of Chriſt
being his holineſs, he is ſatisfied with him ; and
as he is in Chriſt, and Chriſt in him, he ſtands
holy to God : without the conſideration of his
own righteouſneſs, which is according to the law,
either in an active or paſſive ſenſe.

Holy and without blame before God in love :
unto this we were choſen in Chriſt before the
foundation of the world," Eph. i. 4.   True holineſs conſiſts in a conformity to the nature and
will of God ; without which we cannot ſee him :
nor will his preſence (to us) contain the fulneſs
of joy.   Chriſt is made of God unto us ſanctification : Chriſt, including the people in himſelf,
in all his doings and ſufferings, ſanctified himſelf, that he might ſanctify them : which he effected by the offering up of his body once for
all.   Through the whole ſcene of his humiliation,
Chriſt was conſidered as the ſole ſinner, whoſe
purgation, by adequate chaſtiſements, was the
purgation of the whole : He, through his blood,

being a plenary propitiation for all: hence we read, when he had by himfelf purged our fins, he fat down. Holinefs, in the firft fenfe, as applicable to mankind, intends that ftate wherein Jefus Chrift hath placed us before the face of God: This is our holinefs in the divine account; here the holy eye beholds us with pleafure, and we are entitled *unto*, and bleffed *with* his complacency and delight. This is our legal meetnefs to be partakers (with the faints) of the glorious inheritance.

BUT *this*, is true to them who believe not; as righteoufnefs was to Abraham, when in uncircumcifion : yet, when we come to the faith and obedience of the truth, *then*, what is true in Chrift, is true alfo in *us*. It is impoffible for me to mean a phyfical change ; as though nature ceafed to be itfelf, and the paffions no longer fubfifted. But my meaning is, that Chrift dwells in the heart by faith, as made of God unto us, wifdom, righteoufnefs, fanctification, and redemption : that what is wrought and per-

2   fected

fected in *him*, as our furety and reprefentative, is revealed and manifefted in *us:* until the confcience anfwers to the gofpel report ; or to what is thus wrought in him, as face anfwers to face in a glafs.

THE prophet, as I take it, hath decided the queftion, refpecting diftinction between righteoufnefs and holinefs, as perfected in Chrift for mankind, without their aid, faith, or experience : and the revelation of that grace in them : where he fays, " The work of righteoufnefs is peace, and the effects thereof, quietnefs and affurance for ever." From the knowledge of the *former*, proceeds the *latter* ; therefore, who would grow in grace, muft grow in the knowledge of our Lord and Saviour Jefus Chrift.

THE fcriptures fpeak of faints, as being fuch in Chrift Jefus *only*, and not in *themfelves*, in their own virtues and righteoufneffes. The gofpel fhews us, what we are in Chrift, and what he is made of God unto us. In proportion to faith, and affurance, we appropriate *him* and his

un-

unsearchable riches ; as pertaining to us ; adding
to faith, virtue ; and to virtue, knowledge ; and
to knowledge, temperance ; and to temperance,
patience ; and to patience, godliness ; and to godliness, brotherly kindness ; and to brotherly kindness, charity. For, if these things be in you, and
abound, they make you that ye shall neither
be barren, nor unfruitful in the knowledge of our
Lord Jesus Christ. But he that lacketh these
things is blind, and cannot see far off, and hath
forgotten that he was purged from his old sins.

I AM aware of what men have learned to say
on this subject : they mean to patch the old garment with pieces of new cloth ; by which means
the rent is still made worse : they mean, that
these virtues and graces are to be *personally* acquired, in habit and practice, until their calling
and election be made sure by means thereof.

But I conceive, that all these virtues and
graces are in Christ, and are numbered among
his unsearchable riches. When men have at-
tained

tained to the faith of our Lord Jesus Christ ; to know that they are one with him, and he with them, and follow on to know their Lord ; *then* all the treasures of wisdom, and of knowledge, which are hid in him, open up to their view : and they are authorized to appropriate, what they apprehend in his riches and righteousness : hence, from his immense treasures, they have faith, then add to their faith, virtue ; then knowledge, then temperance, then patience, godliness, brotherly kindness, and charity. " Thus, receiving from his fulness, and grace for grace : until they all with open face, beholding, as in a glass the glory of the Lord, are changed into the same image, from glory to glory, even as by the Spirit of the Lord." Here, they are conscious of their being as Christ is ; yea, even while they are in this present world, compassed about with infirmities, and ever confessing, that in them, according to the flesh, there dwelleth no good thing.

THE apostle, speaking of the holiness of the true worshippers, says, that being once purged, they

they have no more confcience of fins; and that they are made perfect, pertaining to the confcience.

But methinks I hear you complain, that I am not yet in your path : You afk me, whether the believer on Jefus has not fome mark, fome character, to diftinguifh him from fuch who believe not ? I reply, he has : Firft, he has an ear-mark. Nor is it an uncommon thing for a fhepherd to diftinguifh his fheep by an ear-mark. Under the difpenfation of Mofes, the fervant who (from his attachment to his mafter, or love to his wife and children, who were not to partake of his freedom) renounced his privilege of freedom from fervitude, had his ear bored with an awl : it was done in the prefence of the judges, to fignify, that it was his own choice, and that he was under none other compulfion than love, to abide in the family. It was done at his mafter's door, implying, a determined refolution, and vow, to abide in the houfe all the days of his life, to hear his mafter's voice,

voice and to do his will. Again, our Saviour, by the Pfalmift, fays, "Sacrifice and offering thou didft not defire, mine ears haft thou opened :" which opening of the ears, the apoftle to the Hebrews conftrues, doing the will of God: The great Shepherd alfo fays, " His fheep follow him, for they know his voice : and a ftranger will they not follow, but will flee from him : for they know not the voice of ftrangers."

I AM aware of the pretenfions of all who call themfelves, or choofe to be called gofpel preachers, to the above character : All who are but *nominally* chriftian join in the fhout, " We are his fheep, we know, we hear his voice, we follow him ;" but the voice of a ftranger we neither hear nor follow. Yet, as the claimants are extremely various : perfectly oppofite in fect, difcipline, doctrine, and faith : they cannot all be worfhippers and followers of the true Chrift : many of them muft be hearers, and followers of the ftranger, whom they profefs to difclaim.

D d WHEN

WHEN Mofes and Elias in their veftures of glory, attended the Saviour in the mountain of his transfiguration ; and there fpake with him, of his deceafe which he was to accomplifh at Jerufalem ; his difciples, whom he favoured with this bleffed interview, heard the voice from heaven, faying, " This is my beloved Son, in whom I am well pleafed ; hear ye him." Hear him in preference to Mofes and Elias, whom ye were wont to hear : theirs was the miniftry of the Old Teftament, containing the dead and killing letter : but *his* is the miniftry of the New Teftament, which has the Spirit that giveth life.

HEAR the well-beloved Son, for in his deceafe accomplifhed at Jerufalem, the miffions of Mofes and the prophets have their final end ; every prediction, promife, requifite, and threatening, contained in the law and prophets, are, in his death and refurrection, executed, fulfilled, and accomplifhed. Beyond *his* death, there is no curfe ; for he was made a curfe for us : in confequence

fequence of which, we are delivered from going down into the pit. Beyond his refurrection, we are not to look for the accomplifhment of promifes : " For all the promifes in him, are yea, and in him, Amen." Therefore, hear the fpeakings of his blood.

HEAR ye him in all particulars of his humiliation : in his birth ; in his circumcifion ; in his toilfome life, his baptifm, fafting, prayers, and temptation : in his agony and bloody fweat, in his tremendous, yet precious death and burial : in his triumphant refurrection and afcenfion ; and in the coming of his witneffing Spirit. In all thefe Jefus fpeaks light, life, and immortality to man : in all thefe he afferts, and indifputably *proves* the love of God to his creatures ; free, rich, invaluable, unchangeable, everlafting : that their debts are paid, their crimes cancelled ; and that the hand-writing which was againft them, and which was contrary to them, he has taken out of their way, and nailed it to his crofs.

. THIS

THIS is that ear-mark, which diftinguifhes the fheep of our Saviour's pafture : This is that teftimony, which all his *true* worfhippers attend to : nor is it from whim, paffion, fluctuating frame, or tranfient influence of the Spirit of truth himfelf, that they hear him ; but from prin-ciple, from choice, they *know* his voice and fol-low him.

THEY follow him as their great Fore-runner, who went before to explore the dangerous pafs : where they perceive *his* track, they follow with-out fear : no open oppofition, hidden ambufh, nor fecret fnare have they there to fear. They are perfectly affured, that he has not only, as their Fore-runner, minutely and critically examined every difficulty ; but that, as the Captain of their falvation, he has removed them all out of their way, and has rendered their path to glory, fo direct, fo fecure, that the *wayfaring man,* though a fool, fhall not err there'n.

THEY

THEY follow him as their Shepherd, on whofe watchful care they are dependant : no obftacle appals *him*, nor will he forfake them in the face of danger : but, from the experience which he learned by the things which he fuffered, from his knowledge, by which he juftifies many ; from his love, tendernefs, and power ; he continues to be their Saviour, through all the diftreffes of life : as he has already been, from every pain and penalty incurred through their offences ; by laying down his life for them.

THEY follow him, not for the meat which perifheth, but for that which endureth unto everlafting life : by him they go in and out, and find pafture, and have that to eat which the world knows nothing of.

BUT, probably, you will afk me, Do they not diftinguifh themfelves by following his footfteps ? Undoubtedly—they follow and appropriate every footftep which he hath trodden ; hence, what he *is*, what he hath *done*, *fuffered*, and obtained

by

by means thereof, is *theirs:* and as they are righteous in his righteoufnefs, fo are they holy in his holinefs : in his Sonfhip they have their adoption, and in his acceptance they have everlafting falvation.

POSSIBLY your meaning is, that the difciples of Jefus are capable of *imitating* him in fpirit and manner. This I cannot fubfcribe to, except ye call fire painted on the wall, an imitation of fire burning in the furnace ; or a pleafant picture devoid of fpirit, reafon, and life, an imitation of *man,* angel, &c. Yea, even *thefe* approach their original, nearer, *much* nearer, than men or angels in their moft fpiritual imitations, can approach to the perfections of Jefus, " Behold, he putteth no truft in his faints, yea, the heavens are not clean in his fight. How much more abominable and filthy is man, who drinketh iniquity like water ?" The facred book fays, " He charged his angels with folly :" and again, " To which of the angels has he faid at any time, Thou art my Son ?" and again,

fpeak-

speaking to the Son, " Thou haft loved righteoufnefs, and hated iniquity ; therefore God,
even thy God, hath anointed thee with the oil of
gladnefs above thy fellows : Again, when he
brought his firft begotten into the world, he
commandedall the angels toworfhip him." What
then is man, who fays to the worm, Thou art my
fifter, and to corruption, Thou art my mother ;
that he fhould pretend to anfwer to the pattern,
and in perfonal virtues to tread in the fteps of Jefus ! Let every fuch confider the parable of the
pharifee and the publican, who went up to the
temple to pray ; the application is eafy.

WHAT *can* we, what *muft* we think, of fuch,
who pretending to the Spirit and practice of Jefus, are manifeftly the reverfe ? Are we to admit of profeffion, in contradiction to fact ? By
no means, my Brethren : let no man deceive
you : when you fee the proud, the diffembler,
the envious, the covetous, the malicious, turn a
deaf ear to his profeffion of following the example

ample of Jefus : **in not believing fuch you will**
honor your Saviour.

THEY will not follow the ftranger ; they know
not his voice. " Mofes verily was faithful in all
his houfe, as a fervant ; for a teftimony of thofe
things which were to be fpoken after : yet the
fervant abideth not in the houfe for ever ; but
the fon abideth for ever, and was counted worthy of more glory than Mofes ; inafmuch as he
who builded the houfe, hath more glory than
the houfe." Chrift, and his gofpel, fuperfedes
Mofes and his law ; therefore, the voice and
lead of the latter are thofe of the ftranger,
which the true worfhipper of Jefus will neither
know nor follow.

THE ftranger may alfo intend the fuggeftions
of corrupt nature ; which every true difciple
of the Lamb is to turn a deaf ear to. We are
fimply to attend to the revelation of God, which
teaches us to " reckon ourfelves dead indeed
unto

unto fin, but alive unto God by Jefus Chrift our Lord." Again: It may intend the devices of fatan, which the chriftian cannot be fuppofed to be ignorant of; and therefore they will not hear the ftranger's voice, nor follow his lead. It may alfo be underftood of fuch, who teach for doctrines the commandments of men. Thefe the chriftian ear cannot relifh; they are unfriendly to man: they are not the voice of the father, the brother, the lover; but of the unfeeling ftranger, whom we will neither hear nor follow.

THE true worfhipper of Jefus ftands diftinguifhed in his attachment to his Lord. "To you who believe (fays an apoftle) he is precious." I will make a man, faith the Lord, more precious than fine gold, even a man than the golden wedge of Ophir. The gold of Ophir intends the gold of afhes, or gold without drofs; probably from a country fo fituated to the fun, that the chymiftry of its beams, in conjunction with the dew of heaven, gilds the

E e   moun-

mountains with such pure extractions from their bowels, as to need no artificial refinement, and therefore called the golden wedge of Ophir.

OR, in another sense, it may intend the spirit and fruit-of the sacrifice. In the sacred book, gold is a familiar emblem of spiritual things, of durable riches and righteousness, extracted from the Crucified upon the altar of his cross, and with just propriety, in my idea, called the golden wedge of Ophir, or of ashes.

As to the literal explication of the prophet, respecting the overthrow and depopulation of Babylon; when a male inhabitant should be so very rare, as to be estimated more precious than fine gold, yea, than the golden wedge of Ophir. This, I say, I wave (being to us perfectly un-interesting) for what more immediately concerns us.

But however valuable and precious (as the golden wedge of Ophir) the spirit and fruit of

the

the sacrifice may be, yet the man Christ Jesus is *more* precious still : to all the benefits we receive from his blood and death, the person of our glorious Lord is infinitely preferable. Christ, in his person, is precious to the true worshipper, above all the riches of his salvation. The nearer we approach the throne of God and of the Lamb, the more fully we come into the spiritual life, the more sweetly we relish, and sincerely join in, the new song, " Worthy is the Lamb," &c. Forgetting ourselves, and all our own happinesses, we are caught up into the admiration of his person, as fairer than the sons of men : the beauty of holiness, the Prince of the kings of the earth.

WHEN the scriptures speak of the blessed man, Christ is intended : and when they speak of the miserable man, they still mean Christ. I am aware of the offence that this assertion will give to many; for here, when man would introduce himself under some particular character,

Christ

Chrift is always in his way. Are you ambitious of the character of the bleffed man, who walketh not in the counfel of the ungodly, nor ftandeth in the way of finners, nor fitteth in the feat of the fcornful? No fooner do you prefs towards the chair, but the gofpel fhews you it is already filled with Jefus. Difappointed in your aim at the higheft character, under which you could claim the love and favor of God as your juft due; you refolve for that of the miferable, as what will entitle you to the compaffion and mercy of your God: preffing on to that feat, not fufpecting a competition *there*; the Spirit of truth, with pointed finger, fhews you it already filled with Him, whofe countenance was marred more than any man's, and his vifage more than the fons of men.

WHAT! fay you, is Jefus every-where? is Jefus every thing? is he the higheft? is he the loweft? is he the bleffed? is he the curfed? Indeed, my brethren, he is: He fills all things; he is the firft, he is the laft, the beginning and

the

the end: O! he is all and in all: and you, and I, are nothing but by him. This, my brethren, is the glorious Man, more precious than the golden wedge of Ophir.

AGAIN, the true worſhipper abides in the ſimplicity that is in Chriſt. Simplicity hath divers acceptations in common language, and even in the ſcriptures: ſometimes it intends ſilli-neſs, foolishneſs, indiſcretion, &c. at other times, it implies ſingleneſs of heart, plainneſs of ſpeech, plain dealing, and artleſs honeſty. In the *latter* ſenſe, the apoſtle intends it: where he ſays, " in ſimplicity and godly ſincerity, not with fleſhly wiſdom, but by the grace of God, we have had our converſation in the world; and more abundantly to you-wards:" And again, " Leſt your minds ſhould be corrupted from the ſimplicity that is in Chriſt."

CHRISTIANITY, at preſent, reſpecting faith and practice, ſeems to be ſtripped of its ſimplicity; and to have none other adornings, than

the

the trappings of human wisdom, and the inventions of men. Faith is *now* a science, unto which, none but men of extraordinary genius can attain. The poor fishermen of Galilee would stand no chance, in the present day, to come to the unity of the faith ; intricate, spruce, and finical as it is : for, as it is scientifically taught, the technical terms must be first gained, and applied with propriety, or whatever a man's conceptions may be, he will not be considered an adept in the faith.

There are also faiths many, such as the faith of adherence, reliance, dependence, assurance, and many others whose names I have forgot. There are also many *acts* of faith, as the reflex act, the direct act, &c. It is also supposed that there are habits of faith, when faith itself is wholly dormant, or out of exercise. To the latter, some impute what they call the final perseverance of the saints : and by this means account for Peter's continuing in the faith, even while he denied it. But you and I, brethren,
are

are unacquainted with thefe prodigious fineffes, we are fimple enough to think that there is but one faith; and that no man has faith, longer than he has it: and that *that* faith which is not alive, is dead: and that our perfeverance and prefervation to eternal life, is *in him* and wholly depends *upon him* who fays, " Becaufe I live, you fhall live alfo."

As to what in the prefent day is called Practical Chriftianity; with the fame tongue blefs they God, even the Father: and therewith curfe men, who are made after the fimilitude of God. Holy mortified faints of a long ftanding, who have been long dead to the world, whofe converfation is in heaven, and who have indeed one foot in the grave; the eclat of whofe harveft-home, we have been taught to expect, and look for; when they fhould be gathered into the garner, as a fhock of corn fully ripe: during thefe our expectations, they have, in their laft moments as it were, been dabbling in politics; ftudying hireling authors, and racking their inventions,

ventions, to prove the *utility*, and even the *equity*
of oppreſſion : and, under a pretended voice of
peace and friendly advice, ſtimulating to war
and human blood-ſhedding.   O rare modern
apoſtles ! O rare practical chriſtianity !

Does not the above feed infidelity, and give
men cauſe to ſay, that the chriſtian profeſſion is
merely a farce ? Their pretended maſter (ſays
the objector), according to them, was holy,
harmleſs, undefiled : and his diſciples, particularly his miniſters, profeſs to walk in his foot-
ſteps : but we perceive them to be men of this
world, fond of riches, honors, fame and power ;
not in any degree ſuitable to their profeſſion.
I am obliged to confeſs, that, from an *impartial*
view of the holy men of the day, they have juſt
grounds for their objection.

The ſpiritual worſhipper meddles not with
politics, he delights not in war, his Maſter's
kingdom is not of this world : whatever nation
his country may be at war with, it is impoſſible

for him to faft and pray for the deftruction of either : but that they fhould live in peace, concord, and, as brethren, together in unity, is the appetite of his foul : for *that* he hungers, thirfts, and prays, according to the Spirit of his Saviour. This, my brethren, is chriftian fimplicity.

As to modern faith, who can comprehend it ? More juftifications, and methods of effecting them, have been found out in our days, than men or angels knew before : or than they who ftand before the throne of God and the Lamb, will ever know. Yea, according to the prefent fyftem, fuch architecture, fuch a building, is required of who would be thought a chriftian, as Milton defcribes in his bridge : not fuch a one as Trajan built acrofs the Danube, or a bridge acrofs the Atlantic, from Great Britain to the American ftrand ; through which, though wide and deep, a bottom may be found : but a bridge over the bottomlefs abyfs, in emulation of the Creator of all things, when on the empty air the earth be balanced well.

WHAT is not true, until it is believed, affords no foundation to build upon : it is drawing the line, or plummet, over chaos ; and laying the foundation upon fpace. And yet, that God loved us, and laid the iniquities of us all upon Jefus, that Jefus died for our fins, and put them away by the facrifice of himfelf ; though preached in the gofpel, is not (according to modern fyftems) true until it is believed. Thus man's faith is made to give virtue and dignity to the blood of Jefus, and what renders it propitiatory for fin. Yea, Chrift himfelf is formed by faith, if we are to believe, that " an unapplied Chrift is no Chrift at all."

You and I, my brethren, cannot but perceive, that thefe diftinctions are all calculated

3   to

to render man coadjutant to the Almighty : that, as allies in the fight, they may divide the spoil, and share the glory. But this, to us, is not only inadmissible, but abhorrent : it stands in direct opposition to the simplicity that is in Christ, wherein the true worshipper abides with joy and thankfulness.

THE simplicity of salvation, which is *in* Christ (as already hinted) intends a free and *full* salvation wrought in *him* according to the will, wisdom, and power of God : and, all without any virtues, pains, or penalties, by us personally atchieved, or endured : In the simple, or implicit belief of this, as the revelation, or word of God; consists the simplicity of the faith ; in the power and spirit of which the disciple of Jesus abides : not judging himself by himself, nor comparing himself with himself. This faith is one ; it cometh by hearing, and hearing by the word of God. It gathers not from *man*'s doings,

suf-

sufferings, frames, nor feelings.; but fortifies itself wholly in the faithfulness of God, and rests itself upon his word. And this it does at *all* times, and in *every* condition of the heart. " Faith is the evidence of things unseen, and the substance of things hoped for." " Although the fig-tree shall not blossom, neither shall the fruit-tree be in the vines; the labour of the olive shall fail, and the fields shall yield no meat; the flock shall be cut off from the fold, and there shall be no herd in the stalls; yet will I rejoice in the Lord, I will joy in the God of my salvation."

THE faith of Christ hath also a simplicity of manners; the spirit and power of that gospel, which the true worshipper believes, instructs and influences him to consider all mankind as his brethren : hence he cannot *wish* evil to his neighbour, much less can he defignedly *injure* him.

To

To follow peace with all men, is his fentiment, aim, and defire : knowing that Chrift
his Saviour gave himfelf a ranfom for all, to
be teftified in due time.

Brethren, farewell.

   Your Brother and Servant,

   (for Chrift's fake)

        J. R.

F I N I S.